The WRATH of DOG

The Chained Gods Series Book 1

Tamira Thayne

Chained dog photo (used on the cover) courtesy Darin Ashby, dashdezigns.com

Published by Who Chains You Publishing
P.O. Box 581
Amissville, VA 20106
www.WhoChainsYou.com

Cover Model: Brynakha Vaettir

ISBN-13: 978-1-946044-06-8
ISBN-10: 1-946044-06-7

Printed in the United States of America

First Edition

❖

To my daughter, Brynakha
I love you just as you are,
even without magical powers.

Also by Tamira Thayne

AUTHOR OF

The Wrath of Dog: The Chained Gods Series Book 1

The Curse of Cur: The Chained Gods Series Book 2

The King's Tether: A Chained Gods Series Prequel Story

The Knight's Chain: A Chained Gods Series Story, Vol. 1.5

Foster Doggie Insanity: Tips and Tales to
Keep your Kool as a Doggie Foster Parent

Capitol in Chains: 54 Days of the Doghouse Blues

The Animal Protector Series:
Smidgey Pidgey's Predicament
Spittin' Kitten's Speed-Away
Raffy Calfy's Rescue

EDITOR OF

More Rescue Smiles: Best-Loved Animal Tales
of Resilience & Redemption

CO-EDITOR OF

Unchain My Heart: Dogs Deserve Better Rescue Stories
of Courage, Compassion, and Caring

Rescue Smiles: Favorite Animal Stories of Love and Liberation

Contents

Chapter 1: Wrath

The hairy beast growled and lunged at me, his rusted logging chain straining to break—like it did every morning I cut down his back alley.

"I need to find another way to school," I grumbled to myself, heart pounding as I looked away and shuffled past him. No reason to deliberately provoke the Wrath of Dog, my oh-so-aptly-dubbed title for him.

Truth be told, I pitied the thing. "What kind of asshat chains their dog outside?" I furthered my inner rant.

At the age of 17 (and a half, thank you very much) I already had a heart for the animals, a trait pounded into my head by my bleeding heart mother from the time I could walk.

I could go on and on about dogs and chaining, Mom's monologue was just that stuck in my brain. "Dogs deserve better than life on a chain," she'd fume and fuss each time we passed a dog like Wrath.

Yeah, Mom, I get it. Someday I'll free Wrath and we'll rise up and smite his nasty-butt owner. For today, though, I just need to get past him without dying and make it the two blocks to class before the bell rings and I have another detention headed my way.

Sometimes it sucked to be me.

But never as much as it sucks to be Wrath, my do-gooder conscience—sounding suspiciously like my mother—reminded me.

Gah. Where was a dog biscuit when you needed one?

With one last glance to make sure the chain was holding, I took off at a run through the remnants of yesterday's skiff of snow and up to the doors of the high school.

Wrath's plight was soon forgotten.

"Bay!" the cheery scream echoed down the corridor. I cringed, my introvert soul longing to slink away unnoticed. But my Leo best friend would have none of that as long as she was still kickin', above ground, and had any air left in her lungs to bellow.

My exact opposite in every way, Amaya was short to my tall, loud to my quiet, and blond to my brunette.

She was curvaceous, cute, and sassy, whereas I was willowy and somber, with more of a girl-next-door thing going for me. Lucky me.

We shared a love of snark, all things fur-covered, and a devotion to each other that went beyond the high-school best friendships that were here one day, gone the next.

I did adore her.

But maybe not today. Today I wanted to turn and flee as all eyes in the crowded pre-first-period hallway swept my way. "Amaya, what in all Holy Hades?" I grabbed her arm and steered her in the direction of the biology classroom.

"Why can't I sidle into class even one day without all the dramafest?" I complained, rolling my eyes skyward and silently begging for a little understanding of my simplistic, hide-under-a-rock personality.

"Um, because I'm me. And I consider it my solemn duty to haul you out from under your bad hairdo and don't-look-at-me clothes and integrate you into society, Little Miss Scaredy Cat," Amaya smirked and flung her blond mane over her shoulder. Then she lowered her voice. "Speaking of cats, did you remember that Old Lady Dotson has us dissecting a cat in biology this morning?"

"WHAT!" I shrieked. "Oh, Hells to the No!" I might be shy and definitely not a wave-maker, but if you are messing with an animal? Look out. The gloves come off.

I straightened, my inner warrior clawing to the surface. Dragging Amaya behind me, I marched straight through the classroom door and up to Ms. Dotson's desk, demanding to know if this was true. "Do you really expect us to skin a cat in lab today? A CAT? The very same companion animal living in millions of homes across America? The same pet curled up on my bed at this very moment and calling himself BooBoo? Please, tell me it ain't so."

I was so ticked and incredulous I was babbling and quaking in my boots, literally; I was rocking to and fro in my faux-leather Doc Marten knockoffs, which today I thought I'd smartly teamed with my favorite pair of worn skinny jeans.

I realized I probably looked ridiculous making a scene in front of the whole class—fists clenched, steam rolling out my ears, and still sporting the green ugly winter jacket my mother forced upon my personage this morning.

Great! I could've at least stopped by my locker before taking on the world.

I personally preferred to go with the goth or emo look, but

Mom got a little crazy when I tried to wear too much black to school, so compromises had to be made. Hence the green puffy coat.

Ms. Dotson, who wasn't called Old Lady Dotson behind her back for nuthin', merely gazed down her nose at me, sniffed, and smoothed her graying hair before lashing out at me. "Ms. Valec! That will be enough out of you. Yes, we WILL be dissecting cats in the lab today, as I informed you yesterday. Was your mind elsewhere again? As I said, if your so-called cat BooBoo has white fur, merely choose one with black, or vice versa. Otherwise, you can expect to enjoy your second visit of the week with Principal Baird. Your choice."

Holy furballs, word travels fast, I thought to myself. I'd just gotten my first detention yesterday in gym class, and already news had spread through the faculty lounge. It wasn't MY fault, of course, and in my defense I had made it through December without incident. That nasty skank Denise had cornered me behind the bleachers during the volleyball game, taunting me about my mother's latest activist arrest.

Mom was widely known for her vocal defense of animals, and more than once it had ended with her being hauled off in the paddy wagon. She believed that the animals and those who stand for them have very few rights in this world, while those who tortured, neglected, and abused our furry friends most often got off scot-free.

I loved her, and was proud of her for standing up for her convictions—I *was*. It was just that sometimes the fallout fell out in *my* direction. As a teenage girl trying to slide through senior year without any major brouhaha, I was all too often put in the position of either defending Mom's honor or saying nothing while Denise and her ilk called her a criminal and worse. It sucked.

Not that Denise Cohan was Senior Class royalty or worshipped by the Page High masses. Far from it. As the school bully, at about 5'10" and 250 lbs., she was far more feared than revered, and I just so happened to land into her victim-of-the-week spot on one too many occasions.

"I hear your mom's a dog thief now," Denise had derided, lip raised in a sneer, greasy brown hair straggling into her eyes, finger poking me in the center of my chest. "She's nothing but a common criminal. I gotta make sure all the other peeps in gym class don't leave any valuables laying around, cause I'm sure the apple's not fallin' far off that family tree."

Huh, maybe I *was* an apple, because all I saw just then was RED. Normally I keep all the pain inside, pretending the insults don't get to me, but yesterday I'd felt the flush of anger start at my toes and quickly work its way up my body to heat my face.

Before I could think better of it, I charged Denise and shoved her into the back of the metal bleachers. I was as shocked as anyone when she flew off her feet and landed on the bottom rung, her head making a sickening thunk before she rolled off to the side and lay crumpled at my feet.

Oh no. What have I done?

A moan interrupted my horror-filled visions of a murder conviction and subsequent lifetime imprisonment at the tender age of 17. *Thank the Goddess!* I never thought I'd be happy to see the school bully alive and well, but damn, it was good to see Denise pulling herself up that bleacher step…a little worse for wear, but nothing a good night's sleep or two couldn't fix right up.

A knot was clearly visible above her right temple, but there was no dripping blood or gaping flesh wound to deal with.

Luckily for me, her posse had quickly scattered, but Melody—one of Denise's other bullying victims—witnessed the whole shit-show and refused to leave my side during the inevitable trek to the principal's office. Melody insisted that Denise had started the brawl and I was just defending myself, and maturely asserted herself with the school authorities in a way that I both admired and envied. *What's gotten into her?*

Denise and I were equally gifted with Saturday detention for fighting on school property, but it was better than I could've hoped for given the circumstances. I'd take it.

Now here I was the very next morning faced with another impossible choice: cut up cats, which I was unequivocally morally opposed to, or face another detention—or worse, suspension.

Bah. Sometimes I wished I was oblivious to right and wrong like most of my fellow students appeared to be. Curse my mother's social mores and Dotson for being an unfeeling wench.

And, curse me for what I knew I was about to do.

I stood straighter. "I absolutely refuse to skin, dissect, or otherwise mangle a perfectly good cat who deserves our respect in death, even if no one gave him or her the proper respect in life, Ms. Dotson."

Dotson, obviously done with our discussion, merely pursed her lips, shook her head, and pointed toward the door.

Amaya, who'd been rooted by my side during the tirade (in classic-BFF solidarity), grinned and bowed to my animal-activist prowess.

She, being the actor type, projected her voice, making sure

the whole class got a ringside seat to the show. "Ms. Dotson, I don't think I'm in the mood for cutting off Mr. Claw's digits today either," she simpered, examining her nails and playing it up like she was preening for the Oscars. "I just had my own digits done, and—call me crazy—but cat guts just don't belong under this girl's well-manicured tips. I prefer my cats in one piece, alive, and their insides, well, INSIDE where they belong.

"Any of the rest of you chicken livers feel like taking a stand for the animals today?"

She looked dramatically around the room at our classmates, but was met with silence. The 25 remaining students stared sheepishly down at their desks, avoiding eye contact with the trouble twins. Nope, no takers.

Cowards.

Amaya shrugged and turned to me. "Cat solidarity," we shouted, pumping our fists and high-fiving, as we turned and padded out the door, finally getting the chance to put to good use that cat stalking impression we'd been practicing since junior high.

Safely out in the hallway, we fell out laughing, temporarily high from our wicked righteous stand in the face of Dotson's cruelty to animals and the students who we knew knew better. There was definitely something invigorating about taking up for the defenseless, staring down "the man," and refusing to back down.

I didn't regret it for a minute, even thought I knew cats would still be cut up in that room today.

But it wouldn't be because of me.

Unfortunately our high lasted only a moment before the reality of the impending walk of doom to the principal's office reared its shaggy head.

"I'm sorry, Amaya," I whispered as we trudged down the hall. At least I could make that pit stop at my locker now and ditch the hideous jacket of green. "I hope this won't get you in more trouble with the stepmonster tonight."

Amaya's eyes narrowed at the mention of her father's new wife, Robin. She was the stereotypical stepmother dreaded by all children of divorce—a blustery and overweight, overbleached, loudmouth New Yorker who made it her goal to destroy Amaya's self-esteem with weekly groundings, putdowns, and all-around douche-baggery.

The usually-chipper Amaya shrugged and sighed. "Mr. Claws was worth it. It doesn't matter what I do, that woman will find a way to belittle me anyway, so I might as well make it epic." She squared her shoulders, flashed me an evil grin, and marched ahead of me into the lair of the devil, aka Principal Baird.

Chapter 2: Voices

Once in the office, the disgruntled receptionist instructed Amaya and I to wait our turn; we slouched into seats beside the three other students already plunked in chairs along the "Wall of Shame." At just about any time of the day you could find at least two or three kids lined up here waiting for their dose of punishment for whatever petty crime they'd committed against the government—aka the faculty—of Page County High.

I was getting all too familiar with this damn wall.

I leaned my head back against the chair and closed my eyes for a second. I knew Mom would back me up, even storm in here going after the principal and teacher like a banty hen when she heard about their stupid cat dissection program.

But I was just so tired of the drama.

Why did it seem like the only way to stay out of trouble was to quietly do the awful things any normal human *should* consider reprehensible? I didn't get it.

I'd all but nodded off to sleep when I heard a very distinctive, masculine voice in my head that, clearly, wasn't mine. *What the mother of pearl?* I jerked my head up and— trying to maintain my cool facade—glanced around to see if anyone else was acting strangely. Was I was the only one here who was seemingly possessed by aliens?

Or certifiably batshit crazy?

Amaya was busy entertaining the other peeps ahead of us with a highly-embellished version of our animal rights "act of defiance," and being shushed by the secretary. Nothing unusual there.

"Why I NEVER!" came the outraged and distinctly British-sounding voice in my noggin again. "Come on, chaps, time for us to take our leave. I've learnt more than I need to know about today's humans. I can see ones such as these will be of no assistance to us in this war, if this is the way they treat the animals they claim to love. Off we go then!"

Eyes wide, I sat up straighter and seriously tried not to freak the eff out.

Then came the screams.

No, not mine, although if I had any sense I too would have been screaming lustily. It sounded like these panicked shouts were coming from one of the classrooms down the hall, and I could swear that was Carly Ervins particularly shrill screech I was hearing.

Oh, no. Biology class!

The decibels on the shriek factor increased, and suddenly students were pouring down the hall, bolting past the office windows as if their lives depended on it. Everyone in principal heaven jumped up and raced for the door too, either to assist with the crisis or to save their own skins, depending on job title and/or level of cowardice.

"Baylee, let's roll," Amaya had broken off her tale and was pinching my arm, trying to yank me from my stupor. By now the halls were in an uproar, stampeding students pushing and shoving their way to the nearest emergency exits and front entryway.

"I see those fire drills are finally paying off," I snarked to Amaya, raising my voice above the din to be heard. "Cool, calm, and collected, that's us, the students of Page County High."

She rolled her eyes and joined the crowd charging for the nearest escape route, but I turned instead and bulldozed against the flow. I would know Carly's screech anywhere; I wasn't leaving without seeing what happened in that biology class. Was one of the cats still alive or something?

God help me if that was the case.

I turned the corner to the biology hallway just as the last batch of students whipped past, still shrieking and looking over their shoulders at...*What in the wide wide world of sports?*

I stopped in my tracks, my brain not processing what my hazel eyes were telling me. Directly in front of me stood what I could only assume were the ten supposedly DEAD cats from biology class.

Except they weren't dead.

They were very much alive, and walking on two legs directly toward ME!

I froze.

That male voice I'd convinced myself didn't really exist popped into my head again, only this time it spoke directly to me, his lilting English accent and proper speech hinting at a long-ago era. "Good day, Miss Baylee Valec of Virginia, in today's United States of America. We thank you for speaking out on our behalf this morning when we were about to be rudely disemboweled by the cretins of this bloody institution. Your bravery has identified you to us as the one we seek, and we're delighted to have finally found you. It's been a long journey.

"Could we perhaps bother you for a ride out of this festering cesspool of immorality? We have much to discuss, but I think we'd best be going before they try to round us up again and remove our ears. I've grown rather fond of my hearing, thank you very much, American pigdogs."

I would have smirked at the delicious insults he was tossing in the general direction of my ever-so-esteemed high school faculty and student body if the situation weren't so bizarre; instead, I could only stare at him mutely, mouth hanging open in what one could only assume was a seriously-unattractive way.

"Oh, and yes, where are my manners. Charlie Tafferton, at your service." Apparently the voice projecting into my head came from the Russian Blue standing directly in front of me, given that he then flourished his arm—I mean paw—bowed, and tilted his head as if waiting for an acknowledgement from me in return.

"Oh," I said, flustered with how to respond to a dead-but-undead talking feline. I settled for simple yet unimaginative. "I walked to school this morning, Charlie. But I do live just a few blocks away. Do you and your, er, friends want to follow me there and we can get this sorted out?"

Chapter 3: Reputation

W*ell, hell. What was I thinking, inviting these cats home with me?* This bizarre happenstance might be too much for even my ultra-animal-loving mother to comprehend. I myself had zero clue what was going on; however, the urgency of our circumstances did not escape my keen mind.

Students from other sections of the school were still flocking past and staring in horror at what appeared to be the reanimated corpses of dead felines hanging out in our hallway—with me, the crazy cat-lover, standing in their midst holding a conversation like we were about to sit down to tea.

This won't improve my reputation in the school hood.

I stifled a snicker at the thought of what Doody-Faced Dotson must have looked like when these guys bounced off the tables and started karate-chopping their way through the terrified student body.

I shook myself. *Focus, Baylee! Save the vengeful glee for later.*

Right now I was tasked with sneaking ten walking-on-hind-legs-and-smelling-like-formaldehyde cats out the door of the school and down three blocks to my house without being shot or arrested.

And, I had to pray that my mother wasn't home.

And then, I had to find a safe place to park these creatures in a house already packed with six resident cats and five crazy dogs until I could figure out what in the land of Mars was going on.

God help me.

Charlie looked at my expectantly. "If you're done with your momentary freakout, young lady, shall we consider moving along before the pandemonium dies down?"

I hunkered down next to him and stage-whispered so all ten of his flock could hear me. "Follow me, and stay low. Can you folks run on all fours like normal cats do? That would be helpful right now."

They looked at each other solemnly, probably thinking I belonged in the looney bin (which I secretly agreed with), and then obediently dropped to all fours and padded along after me.

We took off in the opposite direction of the stampeding students, an oddball yet conspicuous parade of hunkered human and beast slinking along like we weren't the cause of the current mayhem. We hugged the lockers on the left and dashed behind a dividing wall and into a dark recess where I remembered there was a seldom-used emergency exit.

I was pretty sure this constituted an actual emergency situation, so we scampered through the door and behind the line of trees at the back of the school, the blaring siren merely blending at this point with the rest of the chaos enveloping Page County High School.

I stopped, scoping out the scenario and trying to figure out the best way to get us out of here without being spotted.

It seemed hopeless. Authorities and school officials were clustered at the front of the school, surrounded by Ms. Dotson and my fellow biology students, who were all talking at once and flailing their arms in agitation. The rest of the student body huddled en mass nearby, staring at the entry doors and waiting to be eaten by the zombie cats who were expected to break through the glass windows and nosh on their craniums any second.

As I scrambled for a solution, along came Charlie's voice in my head, "Leave the distraction to me, and get ready to run in three seconds. We'll follow."

Suddenly a massive brawl erupted in the crowd of students up front, with the whole football team throwing down against the basketball team and the authorities and teachers rushing in to break it up.

Did Charlie make that happen?

Tossing that thought into the ever-growing "later" pile, I sprinted for the alley, ten cats loping behind and beside me, keeping up effortlessly despite their smaller size.

What can't these creepy not-housecats do? I wondered.

I suddenly realized I had a much more pressing problem on my hands. The most direct route home took us through The Wrath of Dog's territory, and we were scheduled to hit his boundary in about ten short seconds.

This was SO not good.

Chapter 4: Standoff

"Charlie!" I spoke urgently but silently in my head, wondering if he could hear me. I didn't have to wonder long.

"Yes, I hear you; I was merely trying to be polite throughout that exhaustive mental wrangling you were laying on the both of us back there," came the now more-somber voice in my head.

Great, now I'd have to monitor my thoughts too. What next.

"Rest assured, I make every attempt to stay out of teenagers' minds as much as I can," Charlie comforted me, like *that* wasn't really an insult. "I simply had to know what you were thinking in order to convey it to the rest of my clan. They can't hear your thoughts the way I can, so they rely on me to pass along pertinent information. What's this you were saying about a dog now?"

But it was too late.

The Wrath of Dog gave a ferocious growl and strained at the end of his massive logging chain, every hair on the back of his neck and spine standing at full attention, every muscle in his powerful neck, back, and legs fully poised to spring into action. This was it.

Every hair on the back of my neck stood up in matching

salute.

We were all gonna die.

Charlie paused mid-stride, looking confused, and lifted his nose into the air, taking a deep sniff in Wrath's general direction, seemingly unthrown by the dog's menace.

That wasn't at all the reaction I was expecting, and my adrenaline rode a wave that crashed over me for the second time that day. I was lucky I was young and healthy, or I clearly would have suffered a heart attack what with all the insanity going on around and about me.

"Whaaa-t?" he muttered, puzzled. The tension in the atmosphere dropped a notch, as his failure to either fight or flee the slathering chained threat in front of us left everyone unsure how to proceed with the standoff.

Wrath himself backed up, put his nose to the ground, and then whined. Literally *whined*. *What the Heebees.*

"Your…Majesty?" came the perplexed question from Charlie. "How can this be?"

I looked back and forth between Charlie and Wrath, who had approached each other and were eagerly taking a few more good whiffs of the air surrounding them.

"That's it, I'm done," I threw up my hands in despair, agitatedly pacing back and forth now, making sure to stay out of biting range of Wrath. I may be questioning my sanity, but I wasn't entirely suicidal either.

"Let me get this straight. You're telling me that not only am I on the lam with a talking cat and his kitty clan, but now the dog who's been terrifying me out of my wits each morning for years is actually a king or something? And, you KNOW EACH OTHER?" Admittedly, my voice was starting to escalate to a level one might associate with maniacal hysteria.

"Calm down, young warrior," came another, deeper, and much more commanding voice in my head. Against my will my body relaxed, my stress cortisones fell to pieces, and my attention shifted from all that was wrong with this disturbing scenario to a feeling of well-being that somehow I knew didn't originate with me. I wasn't that in charge of my emotions, let alone able to turn them from frantic to mellow at the drop of a hat.

Now the bastages are influencing my moods, dammit. And I was helpless to stop it.

I wanted to be worked up over this latest affront, but I just couldn't bring myself to be bothered by it, or by the fact that I had slumped to the ground between Charlie and Wrath, with little thought to personal safety or space. Huh.

I pondered the hole I'd ripped in my skinny jeans sometime over the past hour, and wondered if perchance the universe would give me a do-over on today. I'd earned it, right? Something clearly had gone awry early on and I'd never been able to right this ship.

Maybe if I could go back to bed, I'd wake to realize this had all been a very weird—even psychedelic—dream, and I could trudge into school again and take whatever punishment I had coming from Principal Baird.

Anything'd be better than this alternate reality where I found myself drunkenly laid out on the ground between a cat and a chained brownish-blackish German shepherd while they carried on a conversation in my head.

Yep. Something has definitely gone ever-so-slightly awry. I giggled. And, I was saying yep-pah in my self-talk, I noticed, even putting the little pop sound in the "p". *Oi.*

Charlie peered into my face, concern making his kitty forehead pucker. *I didn't know cats could look concerned.* He lifted his paw and touched my forehead, seemingly feeling for a fever, and I smiled and grabbed his paw, kissing the cute little kitty pads and rubbing them on my cheek, even though somewhere in the back of my mind I had a bad feeling I knew where those pads had been—and it started with a form- and ended with -aldehyde.

Yuk.

"Your Highness, I think you might have overdone the mindgrind a tad," Charlie snorted, yanking his paw out of my hand and away from my kissy lips.

I pouted and tried to give him a scratch under the chin instead, but he gave me a "talk to the paw" gesture and backed away from my drunken teenage butt.

Geez, get ahold of yourself, Baylee! This is getting downright embarrassing with you making smoochy lips at a cat who sounds like some old British dude. Gross.

Wrath gave a deep-throated chuckle that came out more like a growl, stood, and shook out his thick black-tipped fur. "I'm sorry, young one," his voice came clearly into my mind again, and the fog began to ease up. "I didn't realize I'd overpowered you so completely. I thought your own mind maneuvers and blocking gifts would have fully manifested by now." He frowned and paced, dragging the chain behind him.

He put me in mind of a middle-aged professor pacing the library, thinking through the latest academic puzzle and determined to be the one to solve it.

I was just about to beg him to please start from the beginning—or anywhere for that matter—so I could understand what was happening to me, when a loud shout sounded from the mouth of the alleyway. "I see something down here!"

Oh, crap! We were supposed to be in hiding by now! I jumped up, my adrenaline popping my mind and body back into high alert, and quickly sent Wrath a mental message telling him we'd come back for him as soon as it was safe.

"Go, they won't get past me for awhile," he grinned, and I rushed the ten kitty clansmen the remaining two blocks down the alley to my fenced yard, hoping that Wrath would indeed be able to hold off the troops long enough for us to disappear inside.

Chapter 5: Critters

The wooden privacy fence surrounding our backyard might resemble a patchwork quilt due to the many times we've had to shore up our defenses, but she was sturdy and kept our guys in while keeping other guys out—exactly what we needed in a fence.

Looks were secondary in importance to function in the Valec household.

Mom always said that we were supposed to be smarter than our dogs (which I personally thought was a tall order), so if the new foster dog or family member was digging or climbing out, it was our job to figure out why and where it was happening and then take the necessary steps to prevent it from happening again.

This meant we either had to patch the corners, dig trenches and cement underneath the fence line, or add welded wire leaners to the top to prevent the prisoners—I mean canine family members—from escaping.

How such a peace-loving woman could suddenly turn into a military drill sergeant when circumstances warranted continued to baffle me.

Mom took our pet care very seriously. And she had a low tolerance for those who didn't.

Problem was, Mom's worldview wasn't shared by many in positions of authority, and the laws were considerably laxer than was necessary to ensure a companion animal was happy and healthy.

Until laws were changed in favor of the animals, and law enforcement got onboard with both educational requirements for pet guardians (she hated the word *owner*, which I used liberally just to annoy her) and actual enforcement of new and improved laws, people like my mom would continue to be arrested for doing the right thing.

I was obviously headed in the direction of a date with the paddy wagon myself.

Now I was in the company of the illegally-absconded-with, dead-but-undead cats who were considered by law to be high school property, AND making plans to bust free a slavering beast who might eat the whole town once he was loosed from his chain.

That's two theft charges right there. *God help me.*

We rounded the corner at a flat-out gallop while my brain feverishly sorted and discarded plans for what to do when I opened the gate. I normally squeezed my way through ever-so-carefully so my own barbarians didn't get loose and terrorize the neighborhood; but with ten cats in tow, and every second meaning the literal difference between their life and death, time was a luxury I didn't have.

"Don't worry about it, Baylee," Charlie's voice reverberating in my skull took me by surprise, again. I didn't know if I'd ever get used to it, or him using my full name like it was some kind of royal proclamation. "I'll use the same kind of distraction tactic I used at the school."

"Um, we can't have our dogs fighting, Charlie, or we'll

have to add an emergency vet trip into our already over-full schedule," I snarked, admittedly feeling a little overwhelmed and anxious.

"I'm just going to project an idea into their minds that there are treats for each dog on the opposite side of the yard, nothing sinister," Charlie continued. "They'll run over to investigate while we slip by and into the house for safety."

Whew! Thank Dog someone had his head screwed on straight around here. "Good thinking, Charlie. On three, then..."

I flung the gate open at the same exact second that five dogs turned in bewilderment, gazing under the tree in the corner of the yard and raising their sniffers to catch the scent of yum-yums their brains told them were waiting in that direction. As one, they trotted to the tree and began to investigate.

"Hurry, Baylee, clanmates," Charlie was gritting his teeth. "I can't hold their attention for much longer. We've got to get inside and fast."

We raced for the door and made it to safety just as the dogs barked and lunged at the gate we'd come through on the opposite side of the yard. Whoever was investigating the alleyway had made it to our little neck of the woods, and our five-dog pack was letting them know in no uncertain terms that this territory was off-limits.

Now that the immediately danger had passed and I was in a comparatively safe place, I sunk to the floor, the door frame the only thing between me and a horizontal state.

Our dogs filed inside through the doggie door to investigate what I'd brought home with me and how I'd slipped by them unnoticed, but they didn't have access to our entry room, so

I could put them off for a bit.

For now, for just this one moment, I needed to fall apart.

And the rest of the world could go to hell while I did it.

I don't know how long I lay there, slumped against the wall while the cats eyed me expectantly, but I finally gave myself a good mental slap and got my act together. Sort of, anyway.

I stood, clasped my hands in solidarity with my inner coward, and made a general announcement to the room.

"Ok, Clansfolk, or whatever I shall call you feline-inhabiting creatures. Luckily my mom must be out working with clients, or she'd have been all up in our beeswax by now. So follow me up to my room—where we can have some sense of privacy—and then you'll enlighten me on what the bleep has happened, if you are indeed some kind of weird aliens, and where we're supposed to go from here."

We trooped en masse up the back steps to avoid the dogs, who were still panting, pawing, whining, crying, and sniffing at the entry room door, desperate to be part of the festivities and investigate the new arrivals. I couldn't bring myself to go soothe them yet, though; I had much more pressing business to take care of first.

I sent up a Thank You to the Dogs Above for this stairwell, which had just seemed odd to me when we first bought the house. Who needed two sets of steps in a relatively small living space? But once we moved in I'd realized it was a lifesaver; I could slip in and up to my room without ending up covered in dog hair and slobber until I was damn good and ready to face our five lovable but cray-cray canines.

That didn't save us from my cats, though.

While the dogs mostly "owned" the downstairs and the backyard, the cats had the run of the upstairs bedrooms, bathroom, and their own "cat room," which my mom had forced me to help her create (don't they have labor laws for children in America?) after seeing the incredible setup at a local rescue nonprofit. It was wicked cool.

Our cat room may not have been quite as fancy as theirs, but we came pretty darn close, if I do say so myself. We splurged for the high-quality laminate flooring, because everyone knows that cats find the closest carpet to puke on. Gross! We needed easy to clean, and easy to give a quick sweep of the loose hair and escaping litter each day, too. Laminate worked. The litter boxes were under an enclosed cabinet with round holes in both ends, so we could open the doors for scooping and cleaning, but the cats had pooping privacy and the floor wasn't covered in litter.

Colorful perches, steps, tunnels, and walkways exploded from the collection of cat trees and bedding nooks in the center of the room. They even had a walkway to a kitty door and screened-in outdoor patio for summer lounging and to get some fresh air without damaging the wildlife or risking becoming prey themselves.

I loved it. Truth be told, it made me wish I was a cat. I mean, how hard would it be to be one of these rescue cats? Get up, stuff your face, grab a drink from the aerated indoor fountain, and cop a squat; then, meander about the play room, escape to the outdoor area, and catch a long nap in the sun while pondering your final breakout and the carnage you will render once finally free of these silly humans.

Mwahahahaha!

Wake up three hours later, repeat. Seriously.

My mom lived for this stuff. She put mega-thought into the number of rescue animals we could handle that would give them maximum quality of life but not put us through sheer hell in the cleaning and caretaking departments. There was a fine balance.

Because we'd had an ugly incident wherein one of our foster dogs had killed a rescue cat, the dogs and cats now lived mostly separated during the day, and at night one or two of the well-behaved and non-cat-hating pups got a hall pass to come upstairs and sleep with us.

We had worked out a great system through years of trial and error; because of our experiences two of our dogs were always foster dogs waiting for their perfect home, and three were our own companions who we knew, trusted, and loved. This kept our pack relatively stable and our home a little less insane.

We were big believers in gates and pet doors to keep everyone safe and comfortable, and so the main set of stairs had a tall gate at both the top and the bottom to keep the dogs downstairs and the cats upstairs. That way even if the first gate was breached, we still had a backup gate in place for mania containment. It worked.

As we opened the door at the top of the back steps, we were greeted by six sets of feline eyes, rounded by fear and curiosity as they tried to ascertain where these new interlopers fit in.

Oddly they seemed to sense that these guys were not normal cats...or maybe they smelled the formaldehyde, which would be enough to drive away most fur-bearing critters. Growls, hisses, and hackles arose, as my cat family slowly backed up and skedaddled to their safe place, peering out from cubbies and climbing to the highest perches.

Sweet! Less stress for me.

It then dawned on me that Charlie and his friends were technically cats, at least for the time being, so maybe they too needed to eat, drink, and use the facilities?

"Um, Charlie?" I asked.

"Yes, Baylee, while we are in these bodies we need to use the facilities like 'normal' cats." He seemed disgusted by his own statement. "But I'm drawing the line at cat kibble." He then looked at his paws, turning them over as if lamenting the loss of thumbs. "I guess we'll drink water from their fountain as well. Would you mind giving us a moment of privacy to take care of business? And, we will require some raw meat if you have any."

"You're SOL there, Charlie," I explained. "Neither Mom nor I eat meat…we're done with that. We love all animals, so we made a pact over a year ago that we'd stop eating them. But, I do have some canned cat food, I believe it's turkey or salmon or something, if that would be more appealing to you than dry?"

Charlie's eyes widened in horror, but he simply nodded, acquiescing.

Tough times and all that, I guess.

I took myself downstairs to the kitchen, where the dogs were super-excited to see me in the middle of a school day; they immediately took to sniffing me up, down, and all around to see what the hubbub was about.

Nosey bastages. Sniff your own damn booties.

I realized I hadn't eaten yet today either what with all the mayhem, so I grabbed some grapes and dark chocolate chips to munch on while I got their cat food ready. I hoped one can each would be enough for now, because that's all we had left in the pantry.

Oops! Mom would kill me for giving it all away (she liked to save it for "special occasions"), but at this moment death-by-Mom was the least of my worries. I had hungry diners to deal with.

Chapter 6: Disappearance

W hen the eleven of us were finally fed and curled up in various spots around my smallish but cozy room (good thing they were cats, I would never have fit ten grown men in here with me—*but it might have been fun to try! Get your mind out of the gutter, Bay. Plus, Charlie can probably hear this thought. Ew.*)

We'd bought this house five years ago when we'd unexpectedly come into a bit of money. Mom's work as a graphic designer had paid the bills, normally, but we were never sitting pretty. She had often fretted over whether we could pay the next month's rent and keep our six-year-old car in running condition, stuff like that.

The financial worry made me never want to be a grownup. She tried not to drag me into our money problems, but I loved her and I could read between the lines.

She had clients all over town and over the internet too, and she was always off to some meeting or another, making presentations, and attending town functions to stay on the radar of the major players in our little pond of a community. I was proud of how hard she worked and I hoped her advocacy for the animals didn't affect her business—even though I knew it was a sacrifice she was willing to make.

She enjoyed her work, but her love for animals was her passion.

It had always been just the two of us and our pets, for as long as I could remember. She wasn't forthcoming about my father, just assuring me she'd been deeply in love with him and that I was wanted by both of them; but then one day he'd just disappeared from her life, and she'd never seen or heard from him again. That was only two months before I was born.

She'd searched for years, even hired a private detective, but always came up empty-handed. All leads had run dry. She looked sad when I'd bring it up, so I learned early on not to ask too many questions. I hated seeing her unhappy.

Then one day we got a notice from a bank neither of us had ever heard of. It wasn't local, that's for sure. A quick google search revealed their main office was located in California, but they had branches nationwide and did a lot of business over the web.

The correspondence was made out to Candice Valec and had an official look to it. At first Mom thought it must be some kind of scam, and was about to shred it without bothering to open it. But she decided to take a quick look just in case, and found out that she was listed as the next of kin on a bank account owned by Randulf Essene, my father.

I had already known his name, at least.

The letter went on to say that the accountholder had left very strict instructions that if there hadn't been activity in the account for twelve years the bank was to close the account and transfer the money to Candice.

My mother gasped, held her hand over her mouth, and sat heavily onto the couch. I remember the moment vividly—

even though I was only twelve at the time—because it was that moment that took the last glimmer of hope from my mother's eyes. Now we had no choice but to assume the worst—that my father had died without me ever knowing him and without my mother getting to say goodbye.

Mom's shoulders shook, and she quietly grieved for the man who was forever lost to her, to our little family. I sat awkwardly beside her, putting a tentative arm around her back and laying my head on her shoulder. I wanted to comfort her, but I wasn't good with outward shows of emotion, and I was at a loss for words.

I knew I should be grieving too, but it's hard to mourn the loss of someone you never knew. I *had* always felt sad that I didn't have a daddy who treasured me like some of my classmates did, and for me this letter confirmed that my dream would never happen for me. That was the loss I mourned most.

I remembered how I struggled with jealousy when I was little and saw the other kids running into their father's arms at the end of the day; I'd wonder, what's wrong with *me*? Why don't I have a father who would love and protect me the way these children did?

The letter went on to explain that we were the beneficiaries of a little over a half million dollars and some change, courtesy of my father. It was obvious that he'd cared enough to make sure Mom and I had something if anything happened to him, and that changed the way I thought about him; and maybe even the way I thought about myself.

Maybe I WAS lovable after all; maybe he had wanted us, hadn't willingly left us. Maybe, just maybe, something awful had befallen him, and he saw it coming in time to make arrangements for my mother in the event of his disappearance.

It sure raised a whole shite-ton more questions that had no answers.

But, a half million dollars?!!

Mom was just as shocked as I was. We were afraid to hope that it was really for reals, because we didn't want to be disappointed again. However, within two weeks the money had been wire-transferred into my mother's bank account, and we no longer had to worry if we could pay the next month's rent. We could, we did, and that part of the whole affair felt good.

We held a private ceremony, just Mom and me, to say goodbye to my father and thank him for loving us. Mom framed a picture of the two of them next to a picture of her holding me as a baby, as our way of saying "We're still a family, even if we didn't get to be one here on earth." She kept both photos on her desk in her home office downstairs.

We talked well into the night after we got the money, making plans and giggling excitedly about the Caribbean cruise we were going to splurge on, and spending and re-spending in our minds the $2000 each "fun money" we'd allotted ourselves.

In the end, we bought a mid-size house with an acre, a garage, and a fence for our dogs; we took ourselves on that cruise we'd always dreamed of, and enjoyed a lavish day of shopping with our mad money. The rest we squirreled away, Mom's business now sufficient to cover our monthly bills, vet care for our brood, and pet food.

It was good to know we had a cushion for emergencies, but we tried our best to live on Mom's income and allow our nest egg to grow.

Our #1 requirement when shopping for the home of our dreams was that it have two bedrooms with attached baths. We'd spent enough time sharing a bathroom, and we knew our mother-daughter relationship had a better chance of surviving intact if we each had our own bathroom space as I entered my teen years. As soon as we saw this house, we'd known it was the one—it fit all our criteria perfectly, as if it'd been custom-made for us.

Both Mom and I had bedrooms with attached baths on the upper floor, and there was a third full bath on the ground floor too, which was nice for those odd times we actually had human overnight guests.

My room was the smaller of the two, but I adored it. In it I felt safe and cherished, like I really did have a father watching over me and giving me a big hug before bed each night. My window overlooked the lake on the edge of town, and I would gaze, mesmerized, as the moon rose over the water and imagine my family intact, together and happy in our little home.

At least I had two-thirds of the dream. And a bunch of crazy animals to love, too.

As I looked around at my familiar room and its current feline occupants, I couldn't get away from the feeling that my world was about to change. Forever.

Chapter 7: Revelations

I snuggled on my bed, the red plaid comforter wrapped around me as if to protect me from whatever weirdness was headed in my general direction.

I mean, I was psyched to finally achieve enlightenment in regards to this morning's mayhem, but I was also terrified of what I was about to learn. How was I going to cope with the reality that my reality was not what I'd always believed it to be?

Charlie had taken a catnap (literally!) and was now pacing the room on two legs, a frown wrinkling his cute little brow. Honestly, I just wanted to squeeze him; he looked like a teddy cat, chubby yet squishy and just the right size to fit in my arms.

But I supposed he'd need a bath first, and I somehow suspected he wasn't into being cuddled like a stuffed animal.

Well, it's not my fault he's so adorable, and that his very adorableness lead to errant daydreams of his cushiony squeezability.

I like animals, what can I say. I'd cuddle most of them if they'd let me, but I was smart enough to understand that many would gladly gnaw my face off if I tried, so I was forced to contain my nestling impulses.

Too bad, too. Those gray foxes and raccoons that my mom tosses food to each night over by the lake? A little slice of scrumptious heaven right there.

Charlie stopped and sighed. "Are you done daydreaming about 'my cushiony squeezability' yet, young miss? While I appreciate that you find me oddly attractive, you are right that I have no desire to be squeezed. Or cuddled. My nap did little to sway my apprehensive mood, I'm afraid. We have much to discuss, and so very little time to figure out where we go from here."

"Fine," I mumbled, embarrassed that I'd forgotten once again that he could hear my thoughts. *So creepy.*

Now I envisioned strangling him instead, projecting that visual image forcefully and in graphic detail to be sure it was received on the other end. By the look of horror on his face, I guessed he got the memo.

I smirked. *That was better.*

This time Charlie spoke out loud, which surprised and intrigued me. I didn't know that was possible, and had assumed that because he'd only spoken in my head he couldn't communicate any other way. He was full of surprises.

His voice sounded like a normal male Brit's would, although I didn't know any such men personally, having only seen them on TV and the net. I got why the American girls swooned for the accent, though, it was adorable!

I wondered why he didn't sound catlike, which I imagined would be squeaky and/or persnickety. Definitely not any version of manly that was in my vocabulary. I wanted to inspect him to see how he did it, but I reminded myself to pay attention instead.

I could always sneak up on him later when he was sleeping

and do a full inspection.

His side-eye glare told me he'd heard that thought.

Oops. Nevermind.

"As I informed you earlier, Baylee, I now call myself Charlie Tafferton, but when I last visited this world I was referred to as Charles Tafferton III, former Duke of Gattersby in England. And, I present to you my team." Each stood as he called their names.

"Daniel." An orange tabby stood. I grabbed my iPhone so I could make note of their names and pelt colors. I'd never remember which name went with which cat without some kind of prop.

"Hold on a sec," I said, noticing I had five missed texts from Amaya, who was afraid I'd been massacred by zombie cats and threatened that if I were dead she'd be deep diving into the afterlife to drag my ass back out.

I zipped her a quick line to let her know that I was home and alive, and promised I'd call her as soon as I could to explain what had happened on my end.

I also noticed mom had texted, but she'd have to wait her turn; I didn't know what to say to her right now anyway, and avoidance was my go-to measure in anything mom-related when I didn't have a true or plausible explanation.

I was next introduced to Curtis, a black tuxedo cat, who looked adorable when he bowed. I wanted to give him a little tray with champagne and hors-da-vors, or however you say that fancy word that means appetizers.

Next up was Rebecca and Ruth, who appeared to be twin calico cats, and I knew I'd never tell them apart, at least not in feline form. *Did they even have a human form?* I wondered.

Smith was a sealpoint Siamese who looked like my cat

Cretin (my old boyfriend named him that, don't look at me), and Bradley was a brown tabby who wasn't nearly as pretty and unusually-marked as my BooBoo, but I would be kind and not mention that fact to him. Unless he pissed me off, of course.

Matt and Jake also appeared to be twins, at least in cat form, and were solid black from head to tail. They weaved through and around my legs suggestively and seductively when Charlie introduced them, and I couldn't help but laugh at their antics. I'd have to keep my eye on those two.

And lastly I met a gorgeous long-haired white cat named Tara, who I was glad turned out to be female, because there was not a manly bone in that cat's body.

Each bowed and said a polite "Hi, nice to meet you," or something along those lines, and I was again surprised that each could speak out loud.

Thank Dogness. That will make things easier.

"Ok," I told them, "now that introductions are out of the way and you all seem to know a little about me, how did you get here and how am I involved in this mess? And just what ARE we dealing with, anyway?"

Charlie took the lead again. I wondered if his team could wipe their butts without asking his permission first. *Oh, they don't need to wipe themselves,* I realized, *they can just give themselves a good tongue lashing!* I snorted.

Fine, I'll stop being so snarky, I thought in response to Charlie's withering glare.

I gotta figure out how to block my thoughts from that man. No sense of humor. I didn't care if he heard that last part.

"In answer to the questions streaming through your head, my team and I are not from another planet, per se," Charlie explained, "more like another dimension of this same planet. Our dimension is called Perrin, and we are inhabited by an immortal race similar to humans in appearance, except that we carry additional genetic skillsets and strengths that make us beyond human."

I gaped in shock while he continued. "We've been around much longer than the human race, but are generally forbidden to come to your realm, as it has been prophesied that an Earth-dweller will bring an end to our culture as we know it. In order to protect all we've built in the last millennia, our King banned travel to your dimension after the end of the Renaissance in the 17th Century. That's the last time the ten of us you see here today have been on Earth."

"So, what changed?" I asked, intrigued by the mystery despite myself. "Why are you here now, and why were you masquerading as dead cats in my biology class?" Now I was getting wound up. "Just how in all that is royal did you go from being gods on Perrin this morning to covered in formaldehyde in my bedroom this afternoon? I'd say that might be an appropriate starting point for the next portion of this conversation."

"I'm getting there, young lady. You might want to cultivate some patience," Charlie snubbed, sniffling in irritation.

I glowered and he continued, unperturbed by my attempt at menace.

"When our people saw the state of your world in the Middle Ages, we decided to meddle, one might say. We couldn't take the state of this planet a moment longer—killing each other, pestilence, a lack of morality. As immortals, we had finally reached an age of some form of enlightenment ourselves, and were disgusted with the state of things on your dimension.

We stuck our noses in where they really had no business being.

"In reality it was us, the Perrinites for lack of a better term, who brought the innovations and the progressive enlightenment attained by your world during the Renaissance Era."

"That doesn't sound like a bad thing, though," I said, puzzled. "You gave the people advances in science, medicine, art, and improved living conditions. I imagine humans would be grateful if they knew what the Perrinites did for us. Did something go wrong?"

"You could say that. We immortals were never authorized to breed, or even copulate with the humans. Our intentions were to come here, gift the world with advances in important areas, and then disappear. But there were those who disregarded the order of the King, and it led to our prophetess experiencing a terrifying vision of our world dying, our people losing their immortality.

"We discovered a bloodline had been born here of one of our least-moral representatives, Phoebus, triggering the prophecy and our society's panicked reaction. We hoped if we pulled our people back from your dimension, allowing the bloodline to die out naturally, perhaps we could change the predicted future."

"But it hasn't worked?" I asked, now feeling concerned for his people myself.

"Unfortunately, no. When we pulled everyone back from Earth, the King had our sorceress set up a curse on anyone who defied the order by coming back to this realm and laying with a human. The details of the curse remain between the King and the sorceress to this day, but everyone in the realm understood it wasn't something anyone dared cross. To our knowledge, no one had defied the order since we left in the 17th Century. But then, 20 years ago, something changed."

I was mesmerized. "What!? What changed?" I needed to know!

"There was a birth—it was the male child that the prophecy was based upon. Our Prophetess, Shanti, had another vision of what was to come when he turned of age and it was even more terrifying than the first. Our world was thrown into chaos. We didn't know what to do or to how to save our dimension.

"Miraculously, a year after the second vision, Shanti issued a third prophecy; this one offering a slim chance of salvation for our people. If a female counterpart was born, also of Perrin blood, this child might develop the necessary skills and ability to lead, to fight, to overcome the male's aggression and stave off the death of our dimension."

My head was spinning. "Wait just one unholy second here," I was trying not to raise my voice, but I was scared, dammit. "Please tell me you don't think I'm the female who can take on this unknown male for you? A man who's got at least a couple years on me, has probably been training for this 'bad boy role' his entire life, and who's obviously strong enough to bring down a world chock full of immortals?"

Charlie hesitated, but then simply nodded, sighing.

"Oh, Hells to the No." I jumped up and started pacing— well, as much as I could in the limited space of my room that wasn't overtaken by nervously-eyeing-me cats. "I can barely get myself out the door to school in the morning. Now you're informing me I'm on deck to save a world I've never even heard of, AND—let's not forget—that I somehow come from the bloodline of said world which would mean I'm not altogether human?"

WTF.

I thought I might hyperventilate, if I had a clue what that actually was. I knew it involved a paper bag and some deep breathing, but there was nary a paper bag to be found in my crowded room.

I guess I'll have to hyperventilate when it's more convenient for me.

"Why me? How did you find me? I'm so freakin' confused!" I wailed.

I felt that same sense of calm enveloping me that I'd felt earlier this morning when Wrath was somehow affecting my emotions. I turned on Charlie.

"Stop it. I can't afford to go back into another one of those weird drunken stupors; unless you WANT me to kiss your dirty little kitty pads again?"

He held up said pads in a gesture of surrender. "Fine, I was just trying to get you calm enough so that we could continue."

"Fine, continue," I grumbled, slumping back down onto the bed and wrapping myself in my comforter, arms clenching my midsection.

"After the Prophetess relayed the third vision to our people, the King and the Sorceress huddled with her for days to figure out how to best give our dimension the chance it needed to survive. No one knows what happened as a result of that days-long meeting, but when they emerged, they seemed to have arrived at some kind of difficult decision."

He paused to take a breath, frowning like he was trying to figure out an elaborate puzzle and discovering he was still missing a piece.

"Then the next day, the King and his entourage left the dimension to come to Earth. That was 19 years ago, and he hadn't been seen since. Until this morning."

"Whoa," I whispered. "So The Wrath of Dog—that's what I call him—the shepherd who's been chained and interfering with my daily trip to school for the last two years is really your realm's KING? How in any flippin' galaxy does that happen?"

"I'm just as baffled by that as you are, young miss," Charlie frowned. "I simply cannot understand: 1. Why he's living as a dog, 2. Why he didn't seem to know me when we first met in the alley, and 3. Why he's sitting on that chain when it seems he could easily release himself. He has many special powers and abilities that humans don't; why is he not making use of them?"

We pondered, argued, and discussed the King's situation for a good fifteen minutes, with Daniel, Smith, and Tara even offering up thoughtful opinions and possibilities. *Huh. I guess they are allowed to think for themselves after all.*

"Well, I don't think we're gonna get too far on the King's dilemma without talking to him further, because we're just throwing out wild conjecture at this point," I said.

Yay! "Conjecture" is one of my English vocab builder words, high five to me.

"Of a more immediately pressing concern is why are you all in cat form, how did you end up in my biology lab, and do you or can you change back into humans—er—immortals, or whatever it is you are?"

Given that the school was searching the neighborhood for fugitive undead cats and my mother might drop a load about me bringing ten more cats into the house, we needed to figure out how to turn these ladies and gents into something else, and quick, before even more Hades broke loose around this joint.

Rebecca, one of the calico twins, answered this time. "In our world, we work, travel, and live in teams, teams which are appointed out of our larger clans. Each clan is made up of those who can shift into the same animal, 'impersonate' it if you will, and our animal becomes part of who we are, and we of it. Our team was chosen to lead the search for you because we are warriors, but most importantly we can all shift into domestic cats, which are prevalent in your society. As cats, we are small enough to sneak into and out of areas quickly, we fight well when cornered, and together we make one heck of a combat squad."

"Impressive! " I said. "So why me, and how in bejeezus did you end up in formaldehyde?"

Charlie, by this time, had come and curled up beside me, falling fast asleep again. I hated to admit that I was getting a bit attached to the little guy, even though he was no fan of my vast snarking abilities. I wondered what he looked like as a man. That would be weird, though, given that I just wanted to rub his tummy and scratch under his chin.

Curtis, the black tuxedo with an adorable white stripe down his nose, fielded this reply. "We've actually been scouring the planet for you for over a year, as Charlie mentioned earlier, and it's been incredibly frustrating. Since the King hadn't been heard from for so long—and we knew soon the scion would come of age—our team volunteered to take on the search for you.

"We've had our best seers working jointly with us from Perrin, and they recently provided information that narrowed our search to your Virginia town, Culpeper it is, right?" I nodded. "This morning we had an urgent message from a seer to flash ourselves to a set of coordinates here. When we appeared at the location, we'd somehow taken the place of the dead cats in the formaldehyde, waiting to be dissected. We were just as shocked as everyone in that classroom to find ourselves in that predicament, believe me!"

I couldn't help but stifle another giggle. I wish I'd have seen it, but the mental image was just about enough to send me into a full-blown fit.

"What did Old Lady Dotson do when you jumped up off the table? Did she have a heart attack?" I asked, a tad too hopefully.

Even Curtis chuckled at that. "Luckily for us we can communicate via telepathy, so we coordinated it so that we all jumped off the tables at the same time and rushed the teacher, who was the first one to run screaming from the room. So much for going down with the ship. Those kids would have all been toast if we really were brain-crunching zombie cats."

Who knew Doody-Faced Dotson was such a coward on top of being emotionally stunted. Lame.

Bradley, the brown tabby, spoke up. "As soon as you informed your teacher that you would not be dissecting a cat today, we knew you were the one we sought. Charlie, as our leader, is gifted with an extra-perceptive mind linking ability, so he was able to open a connection from his mind to yours and follow your path to the principal's office.

"And you pretty much know everything that happened after that. Does that help clear any of this up?"

"Yes, except there's one last pressing issue. For now. How

long have you been cats, and can you change back to your other forms? Please? Not only do I feel like a crazy person holding in-depth conversations with kitties while I oddly want to nuzzle them, but the police, the school officials, and the entire town for that matter will be looking for you. Obviously remaining in cat form while we work through our challenges isn't going to fly."

Daniel, the orange tabby who I'd ascertained by now to be Charlie's right hand man, stood and shook himself out. "We've actually lived as cats most of the year we've been in your dimension. We don't enjoy it, per se, but it enables us to move around unnoticed and without all the necessary human baggage like driver's licenses, vehicles, clothing, money, apartments, etc.

"If you don't mind, could you allow us an hour nap, and then when Charlie wakes we can discuss how best to go about returning to our forms and finding clothing, etc.? Unfortunately, when we take on our immortal appearance, we are naked, which is frowned upon in your culture. Most of us are talented enough to create the illusion of clothing for long enough to acquire an outfit or two, but it's always better if we have something readily available to slip into."

Honestly, after suffering three major adrenaline crashes in the space of four hours, a little nap sounded heavenly to me, too. Nodding, I curled up next to Charlie and let the craziness of my world slip away, for just a little while.

There'd be plenty of time to face my new and oh-so-freaky life when I woke up.

CHAPTER 8: AWKWARDNESS

An hour later I awoke next to a naked dude. *Whoa.*
My brain was still foggy with sleep, but my body went rigid, sending "Mayday" signals to my head. I didn't know what this mess was, or how I'd ended up in it, but I knew I needed to get out of it, and pronto.

The male next to me shifted toward me, opened his eyes, and said "Why are you looking at me so strangely, young lady?" In Charlie's voice.

Uh-oh. Awkward!

"Um, dude, you're a man, and you're naked. In my bed. I'm freaking out here. Seriously, what in Hades?" I scooted away from him toward the wall.

Charlie looked down, saw he was indeed male and naked, and instead of acting embarrassed like I would hope one would under the circumstances, merely added an illusion of being clothed, and then let out a loud "Whoop" of joy.

The nine cats scattered about the room in various sleep positions jolted awake as one and—seeing that their leader was human, or immortal, or whatever—gave reciprocal whoops of delight and all started talking at once.

"How did you transform while you slept?" was the general consensus of the questions bandied about in the din.

Apparently this was a bit unusual, even for their leader.

Charlie, as head of his team and somewhat of an overlord or the equivalent on his dimension, was apparently endowed with the most special princess powers of the group. I didn't know what all he could actually do yet, but I knew he could speak in my head, put ideas or distractions into the minds of groups of people or animals, and more readily turn himself to and from his cat form than his teammates. I assumed there was plenty more to discover.

But Charlie was just as baffled as they were. "I woke up unclothed beside young Baylee only a moment ago, having no idea I'd transformed, so I too am a bit stumped as to how it occurred." He looked at me, explaining, "I've never before transformed in my sleep. It takes immense concentration, and a lot of energy. In fact, I'm usually quite fatigued for at least an hour afterward."

He jumped off the bed, stretching and luxuriating at being back in human form. I tried not to eye him up, which just seemed creepy stalkerish, but he was quite handsome for someone I considered to be an "old guy" based on his proper speech and etiquette. He stood about 6'2", was lean but fit, and had silver hair, a bit shinier than his cat pelt. His face was handsome, in a serious, geeky doctor kind-of-way. All he needed was a pair of spectacles to round out the illusion.

"I feel quite fit at the present moment, oddly so!" He exclaimed and looked at me again, suspiciously. "Did you touch me in my feline form while you slept?"

I looked down, sheepishly. "Well, I might have cuddled you. Don't judge me. You're cute and squeezable, like a big gray teddy kitty. I'm used to sleeping and snuggling BooBoo, but he wasn't here—so I made you my substitute cuddlemuffins."

Understanding seemed to dawn on everyone but me. "It was you!" Smith, the sealpoint Siamese, yelled ecstatically and pointed my way with his kitty paw, "your powers are manifesting. When you touched him you helped him transmute into his immortal form."

Everyone was looking at me in astonishment, which made me feel increasingly uncomfortable, like I had a booger hanging out my nose or something. "What?" I said defensively. "I don't feel any different than I did a week ago. What are these powers you keep referring to? I just went to sleep cuddled up next to a cat, and woke up beside a naked man. To my knowledge I had nothing to do with that!" I protested.

Charlie grabbed my hand and held it firmly between his two, closing his eyes for a second while he concentrated. "Yes, I can feel the energy moving through your body. Your powers have indeed awakened, young warrior, and I suspect when combined with mine allowed me to make the switch easily and comfortably while I slept. Astonishing! You must be quite strong. I cannot wait to further explore these abilities."

He thought a moment, and then continued. "Here's my suggestion. Let's endeavor to find some clothing for the others and myself, and then—as an experiment—we will have you make physical contact with each of them and see if you can assist their transitions as well."

I grumbled but acquiesced, afraid I was gonna be a miserable failure, and in front of everyone. *Double awkward.*

Charlie and I tromped up to our attic where my mom had stored my father's clothes, never having the heart to give them away in case he came back. We were able to gather enough outfits for each of the males, and I raided mom's exercise attire drawer for clothes for the three women.

Add that to the reasons I was gonna be in deep doody when Mom got home today. The list was rapidly expanding.

When we rolled back to my room with our arms full of booty, all nine of Charlie's sentinels excitedly lined up for me to jump start their change engines. Lordy! They seemed to have the utmost confidence that I could do this, whereas I had no idea what "this" even was, and was terrified by my imminent failure.

Eager to get this experiment over with one way or the other, I walked up to the orange tabby, Daniel, and plopped down on the floor next to him. I tried to think of the least compromising position for me to end up in if this experiment actually succeeded. I mean, I'm no prude, but seeing seven guys' junk in one day seemed a little bit of overkill, even for a pervy 17 year old.

Which, of course, I'm not.

So I sat perpendicular to the cat, my knees up in a protective stance, my left arm wrapped around my legs, and my eyes averted. "Here goes nothing," I mumbled, trying to give myself some courage. *Good pep talk, Bay.* Feeling silly, I grabbed his left paw in my right hand, sent him "ok, change now" vibes, and hoped for the best.

Nothing happened immediately, but then I started to feel a tingle at the bottom of my toes; the pins and needles quickly worked its way up my legs, blossoming and extending outward when it hit my lower back. I could only liken it to what it would feel like to experience the rise of kundalini, described by our yoga instructor as the awakening of the serpent energy from the base of the spine and unfurling upward.

The energy then blossomed and engulfed my spinal column, flowed down my arm, and burst from my hand into Daniel's body. Then, where I would have expected to zap the poor kitty into oblivion with such a huge energy overload, the power instead surrounded Daniel in a visible orange shield that seemed both protective and nurturing. The shield slowly seeped into his body and fur, finally dissipating with a flash around his green eyes.

We watched, astounded, as his body didn't stop to think about the transformation, didn't hesitate, didn't take its good ol' time. One moment I was holding a cat paw, and the next I was grasping a much larger—and more manly—hand.

Well, damn, awkward X3. I guess I'd better get used to it.

I dropped his hand like a hot pocket (you know, 'cause they have meat in them), scooted back, and looked out my window while he grabbed the pile of clothes next to him and made quick work of dressing himself.

His friends would have high-fived him if they weren't a fifth of his size and had only tiny paws to work with, but he made do with their cheers. It was the thought that counted.

"I feel excellent!" Daniel exclaimed. "Better than I have in years. I think her energy not only transforms us, but sweeps all the exhaustion from our limbs too. You guys gotta take a hit!"

Then Daniel stopped and looked at me with concern. "How are you, though, Baylee. Do you feel ok, are you well enough to continue to help the rest? Maybe you're giving us your energy and running low yourself."

I shrugged. "I don't feel any different, to tell you the truth.

I'm starting to sense the well of energy in my body now that I know what I'm looking for. It doesn't seem to be diminishing, so let's get this over with before my mom gets home and we have even more explaining to do."

I went through the rest of the team, one at a time, and by the end the transformation was coming virtually instantaneously. I would no sooner touch the cat with my intention to transmute them to their immortal form than they stood before me as naked as the day they were born.

They seemed to feel no shame or embarrassment about their nudity, but tried to dress as quickly as possible out of deference to me. Which I appreciated.

If the kids at school could see me now, I'd be certainly labeled the school "Ho" for hanging out with this many peeps in their birthday suits. Course, it might be more acceptable than whatever names were brewing in the rumor mill since I ran off with "the zombie cats" this morning.

How did my life get so bat-shit crazy in the space of one single day?

I was both intrigued and grateful that the team's hair colors resembled their pelts. Daniel had red hair and if he were American I'd think he was of Irish descent. *That will make my life easier.*

Curtis, the black tuxedo cat, had short, black, curly hair with two white streaks down the sides. He was also lithe and lean, the thinnest of the group but with a mocha-colored pretty boy face and big, beautiful brown eyes. He seemed sweet, and I was looking forward to getting to know these beings who I was already considering part of my team.

Rebecca and Ruth, the calico twins, were also twins in human form, and sported multi-hued hair cut at varying lengths. They appeared Asian in descent, and were shorter than me at around 5'4"; they looked pretty badass, though, like they took their workouts and their jobs very seriously.

Smith, the sealpoint Siamese, was blond with brown highlights and blue eyes, and Bradley had brown hair and dark chocolate eyes like his tabby cat form.

Matt and Jake were twins as well, both bearing jet black, curly hair and darker skin, and the thick, ropey muscles of bodybuilders. Even though their looks were intimidating, they had an easy-going banter and warmth that took me by surprise and pulled me into their world.

And finally, Tara, who in feline form was the long-haired white cat, sported straight, platinum-blond hair as a human that was sure to catch every male's eye. In contrast to the stereotype that dogged blonds everywhere, she seemed to match Charlie in scholarly temperament, and immediately set about trying to puzzle out how I had been able to transform everyone so quickly, and what other powers I might have.

I excused myself from the gathering long enough to clean the cat room (and all the extra poop, courtesy of the immortals in the next room, *ew!*), and feed and water the cats and dogs. Taking care of eleven animals and ensuring the place held to a reasonable level of cleanliness entailed at least an hour a day, given no unforeseen circumstances such as doggie destruction or cat pukage. Those all-too-frequent events added time and an extra dash of unneeded stress to my day.

During the week it was my job to care for the pets after school while Mom was out making the dough to keep us all in kibble and canned food. On the weekends she took care of the critters and I got a much-needed break, which I longed for by Friday, believe you me.

Speaking of Fridays, thank Dog for my sake that was today, because it would give me 48 hours to get all this crappola figured out and dealt with before school rolled around again on Monday.

Somehow, I didn't feel confident that two days would be enough to handle this large a load of doody number twody.

No, I did not feel confident about that at all.

CHAPTER 9: THE MOMINATOR

I had no sooner gotten the maniacs squared away—taking time to kiss, hug, and caress each dog and cat for a few minutes so they knew I loved and wanted them despite all the chaos going on around us—than Mom walked in the door.

I would say I just couldn't catch a break today, but I guess I was super lucky she didn't show up much earlier to see me dragging ten cats through our doorway. And, I was mega lucky the school officials hadn't caught us, and that I'd somehow survived the Wrath of Dog not once but twice today.

Oh, yeah, and don't forget that I've acquired new and still-a-secret-from-me powers; I didn't know how to feel about that revelation, so I was letting it stew in my brain a bit longer.

I guess it could be worse.

"Hi, Mom, how was your day?" I put false enthusiasm into my voice, hoping she wouldn't notice and ask questions. I still had no idea if I should come clean about the events of today or not. She was pretty astute and could often see through my BS, but it all depended on how distracted she was with thoughts of work when she got home in the evening.

She gave me a hug, but was looking frazzled. "Ugh, I have to run back out to meet with a client. She's got an important presentation tomorrow and one of our charts isn't right. I've got to sit back down with her and fix it so she has it for her 9:00 a.m. meeting. I'm so sorry, honey. Can you fend for yourself tonight?"

Damn, my luck was *so* holding out!

I squeezed her quickly in return. "It's ok, Mom. I was thinking of making one of those vegan pizzas we bought anyway. I'll just throw that in and you can have some later when you get home."

She ran off to the bathroom to freshen up her makeup and fluff her hair. She still looked great for a 41-year-old; her hair was long and dark, her face open and friendly, and her build athletic while still managing to appear womanly and curvaceous. Compared to my towering 5'8", Mom was of a more average height at 5'5" tall.

Despite the differences in our build and height, we were still obviously mother and daughter. My mane was a lighter brown with a slightly reddish tint, but we shared the same thick, wavy texture and similar button noses. Mom's hazel eyes held a slight slant, which lent her an exotic look, and I liked to hope mine did too. I still thought she was the most beautiful woman in the world, but don't tell her that.

I don't want her to get a big head or anything.

It felt weird being taller than my mom, as I'd literally looked up to her so much as a child, but I guess I took after my father in the height department. She was still my hero, even though I had enjoyed towering over her (and teasing her about it) in recent years.

She grabbed her purse and her laptop, gave me another quick peck on the cheek, and ran out the door, barely taking time to say hi to the pets.

When she was gone I went upstairs and invited the team down to make dinner and brainstorm our next move. I had four more texts from Amaya, and the guilt descended that I hadn't yet made time to call her back; in my defense, I had no idea what to tell her or even IF I should tell her what was really going on. And, I was a crappy liar.

Maybe the gang could help me figure that out over dinner, since I didn't know their culture and what I was even allowed to tell "outsiders."

As it turned out, all ten of them were super-revved to eat human food again. Although the food on their dimension was tasty and healthy, it was much different than our food here. They wanted to stuff themselves with junk food and try all the things they'd missed out on in the past four centuries, excited that our food had evolved so tremendously since that time. I explained to them that this evolution was both for good and for ill, of course, but they weren't swayed by my warnings.

While I worried that the eleven of us were going to empty the pantry (and Mom was sure to notice), I once again decided to let that be a problem for tomorrow.

For tonight, I wanted to watch their faces as they tried pizza, and nachos, and whatever other typically American and gooey foods I could dig up without leaving the house.

We started with the pizza—I had four left so put them all in the oven—and while I was baking them, we tried out nachos with melted cashew cheese and spicy crushed pepper sauce, a fresh salad with all the fixin's and croutons, and a fruit salad Rebecca and Ruth put together. We followed it all up with a batch of freshly made chocolate chip cookies, my specialty.

They became giddy with excitement as they ate, exclaiming and testing and trying each other's concoctions, and even Charlie and Tara, the more serious of the bunch, had huge smiles on their faces by the end of our dinner.

I felt, for the first time in my life, like there was a chance I could have a big family, like a bunch of siblings…brothers and sisters who teased each other relentlessly but at the same time truly loved and cared for one another. I was starting to fit in, and it felt magical.

We had just finished off the last of the cashew ice cream, with me explaining the principals of veganism to them, when the door from the garage opened and Mom burst through, her pepper spray pulled out of her purse and a terrified look on her face. "What in God's name is going on in here? Baylee, come over here. Are you being held against your will, or about to experience death-by-mom for throwing an unauthorized party?"

I guess my lucky streak had to end sometime.

The Mominator was home. And she was not happy.

I rolled my eyes and gave her a look that said "Mom, you're embarrassing me. Cut this shit out."

Apparently, we had our signals crossed, however, because in Mom language that look must have instead meant "I'm being held against my will, please help me."

She valiantly rushed the room, pepper spray flying willy-nilly as she ran, shrieking as only a Mominator can and attempting to dial 911 at the same time, too. She was crashing into teammates, throwing elbows and jabs in a way that was almost impressive, and emptying her canister into the eyes of anyone who tried to contain her.

I would have laughed if I weren't so mesmerized and

horrified at the massive spectacle she was concocting.

Daniel, Curtis, Rebecca, and Ruth were down, rolling on the ground and rubbing their eyes while they screamed "What kind of sorcery is this?"

Smith and Bradley grabbed Charlie and I and huddled in front of us, kindly offering themselves up as protection from the "pepper-spaying-lunatic-from-hell."

That only left Matt, Jake, and Tara still standing, and the three of them were circling The Mominator, attempting to corral her without going down for the count themselves.

They were especially leery of her spraying hand—based on the wails of their friends—and didn't want to hurt Mom with any Jedi mind tricks, so they waited her out until her canister had finally run dry. At that point Tara stepped in from the left and clasped Mom's arms behind her back, effectively becoming her own set of handcuffs.

Now that the dramafest was officially over, I fell out laughing on the floor, and—true confession—almost peed myself I chortled so ferociously. I had to hold my stomach it hurt so bad from the convulsions. Charlie's clan didn't know what to do or think, and the injured still rolled on the floor rubbing their eyes and spouting some new and colorful invectives I needed to jot down to add to my vocabulary.

Mom was indignant by this time, telling me "You'd better start explaining, and fast, young lady. Who are these people? And why are they eating us out of house and home?"

I ignored her until finally my laughing fit passed, and I was left comatose on the floor with Khronos, my favorite cuddle-buddy shepherd/collie mix, sprawled across my belly. I hugged him to me, stalling for time as I tried to think of what I should tell her.

Curse me for having too much fun during dinner instead of figuring out how to handle The Mominator.

"Charlie?" I sent out through our mindlink, hoping he was getting the message. "Little help here?"

Charlie stepped up toward my mother, taking the lead. *Thankee Baby Jesus.*

"Hello, ma'am, allow me to introduce myself. I'm Charles Tafferton III, former Duke of Gattersby, but here in your time I go by the name of Charlie. My team and I have come a long way in search of your daughter. We have reason to believe she is our dimension's only hope for salvation, and that she is actually half-immortal, a progeny of a non-human from a realm you've probably never heard of but is called Perrin."

Um. I guess that's one way of doing it.

He sounded so serious as he dropped the bomb that he'd either have to be telling the truth or a fabulous actor. Mom's mouth fell open, and she collapsed heavily onto the couch. I think she may have been catatonic. *Uh oh. Maybe Charlie's matter-of-fact approach was a little much right out of the gate.* Admittedly, it was a lot to take in.

Still, at least I didn't have to be the one to do it. For that I was grateful.

I sat down next to her. "Mom? Mom! Are you ok? I know this is a lot. Believe me, you have no idea what I've been through already today because of this. But I have very good reasons to trust they are telling the truth, which we can go over when you're ready." Going on instinct, I put my hand on her leg and thought the word "Calm" to see if I too could send the mellow vibe Charlie and Wrath had used on me earlier.

It seemed to work. Mom sat up, pulling herself together,

and latched onto the considerable mental acumen that was her go-to for strength in times of stress. She looked first at me, then Charlie, asking the question which was on all of our minds. "How could my daughter possibly be from another dimension, or realm, or whatever you're calling it? I was only with one man during the past twenty years, and I loved him immensely. As far as I know he was human."

Her voice wobbled, but she continued. "He disappeared shortly before Baylee was born, though, and we haven't seen or heard from him since. His photo is right in my office over here, on my desk. Come see."

She stood and pulled Charlie up and along after her into her home office. I had forgotten about the photo earlier, I could have shown it to the team to see if they recognized or knew my father as a Perrinite. *Duh.*

The rest of us trooped in behind them, squeezing together into her office. Charlie suddenly stopped midstride, exclaiming "No, it can't be! NO. No, no, no, no, no." Now I thought HE was going to be the one to hyperventilate. Apparently I'd need to carry a paper bag around with me at all times from now on.

One by one the rest of the team slipped by me to see the photo, and the murmurs of disbelief and distress escalated.

"What am I missing?" I too was stressed now but had no idea why. "Who is that? WHO IS MY FATHER!" My voice had risen in pitch since no one was looking at me or answering me, and merely continued to mill about and murmur amongst themselves.

Charlie slid into my mother's desk chair, reaching for the photo to examine it closer. "That's him alright," he said, more to himself than anyone else. "Things are starting to fall into place, then."

"Candice," he said, "I may call you Candice, right?" She nodded. "What is this man's name, and how did you meet him?"

My mom got a faraway look in her eye. "His full name was Randulf Essene, as far as I knew, at least. He went by the name Randy. We first met as I was hiking the Appalachian Trail in the fall before Baylee was conceived. I had suffered a bad breakup, and had taken to doing some risky activities in order to cope with the pain and loneliness I was feeling. I was tired of the bar scene, so I starting hiking alone, and even gave skydiving a whirl."

She continued. "I was out on the trail, and was about an hour from my car, but I had underestimated how quickly dusk was descending. I started hurrying, and I'll admit, I was pretty scared by that point. I was seriously rethinking my penchant for thrill-seeking, and terrified I'd have to spend the night out in the woods, alone.

"Suddenly I heard the unmistakable shake of a rattle; I knew there was a timber rattler nearby, but I couldn't see it. I panicked and started running, unfortunately running right into the snake, which bit me on the left ankle."

She shuddered, wrapping her arms around herself. I sidled up to her and started rubbing her back, trying to keep her calm and help her get through the story. "I knew if I didn't get back to my car and find a way to go for help, I was doomed. This was in the days before we carried cell phones with us everywhere, so I was well and truly screwed if I couldn't stay conscious long enough to reach someone. I had no sooner made it to the edge of the parking lot when I tripped over the berm and fell face first onto the asphalt. At that point I passed out. I woke up in the hospital hours later, having no idea how I'd gotten there."

Everyone was listening in rapt attention. "There was a man sitting in a chair beside my bed, the most handsome man I'd ever laid eyes on, and he introduced himself to me as Randulf Essene. He said he had been pulling out of the lot after a day hike in the mountains when I literally knocked myself unconscious 30 feet in front of his vehicle. He examined me, and realized I probably had both a concussion and a snake bite. He quickly got me to the ranger station, and they rushed me to the local hospital emergency room."

She took a deep breath to calm herself, and then finished her tale. "I spent three days in the hospital, and had to have multiple doses of antivenin, but was able to make a full recovery. During that time Randy rarely left my side. We quickly realized we were 'it' for each other; we'd fallen madly in love, and from that point on spent at least part of every day together. He wined and dined me, and within months we were pregnant with Baylee. We were both ecstatic about it, and planned a grand wedding before the birth. But then he suddenly disappeared, and I never heard from him again. I hired a private eye, but the trail just went cold.

"About five years ago we got a letter in the mail saying that he'd requested a bank account to be transferred to my name if he didn't make any deposits or withdrawals within twelve years. At that point we realized he must actually have died without anyone ever knowing or finding his body, so Baylee and I held a small ceremony to say goodbye to the man I loved and the father she'd never gotten the chance to know." Her sadness was palpable. "I just have no idea what happened to him."

Everyone had found places on the floor to sit or lounge as they hung on Mom's every word. When she was done talking I gave her a big hug, never realizing what all she and my father had gone through together in their short time, and how wanted I was by both of them. That part felt good.

"I love you so much, Mom," I said, with a tear in my eye. "Thank you for being here for me all these years when you were suffering so much pain and heartbreak, too. I consider myself lucky to have such a great mom."

There was a small chance I was buttering her up to get out of any trouble for all the missing food in the house, *but I do mean it, too, I swear*, I assured myself.

I just usually wasn't so openly sentimental.

I knew I'd broken about ten of her rules today: no talking to strangers, no bringing strangers home, no giving strangers all our food, no giving strangers my dad's clothes. Yeah, it would be epically harsh if she didn't get a grip on herself and realize I was doing my best with the shitty situation I'd been dealt.

By the man who was slated to be her husband, it appears. So she'd better cut me some slack.

The dogs had crowded their way into the office with us and lounged on the floor with the team, having gotten all their sniffing needs satisfied earlier. Many of the clan members absently rubbed the dogs' heads or bellies, deep in thought, as they tried to figure out what had happened to my father and how this puzzle all fit together.

Finally Charlie spoke up. "Well, Candice, Baylee: I have good news and bad news. Given that my earlier method of delivery wasn't well received by Candice, I wanted to preface this portion so as to ascertain whether you would be able to handle it or not. Shall I proceed?" His British accent was in full force with the strain of keeping himself in check.

I grabbed Mom's hand, and looked at her for her response. She sighed. "Ok, Charlie, go ahead. Give it to us straight. I can't imagine it being any more unbelievable than 'your daughter's not fully human.' But I guess I could be wrong. Hit us."

He appeared shocked. "I have no intention of hitting you! What kind of man do you take me for?"

I giggled. I forgot that, even though the clan seemed to have come to understand a lot of today's slang during their last year chasing around this dimension, there were still idioms they just wouldn't get. "'Hit me' is just lingo we use in the U.S. that means 'go ahead and give it to me straight.'"

"Oh," he said, grinning sheepishly. "Yes, I imagine there are quite a few phrases in your local jargon that I will misunderstand. Thank you for enlightening me. Let me proceed, then. Candice, Baylee, the good news is that your would-be husband and the father you've never met is not in fact dead. He is at this moment very much alive . . . and in this local vicinity."

I was done. Today was just too much. I slumped to the ground beside my mother, who had also fallen to her knees. It was an effort to breathe.

It would not be an exaggeration to say that this day would stand out as the most messed up of my young life. I was so discombobulated that I had no snark left in me, and I prided myself on always being snark-ready. Snark-tastic. Snarkable.

I somehow doubted that no matter how long I lived or what goobers would next hit me from this whole big chaotic bag of snot, no day could ever match today in the "I'm totally effin' freaked out" department.

Hands-down winner.

"So . . ." I drawled out, seemingly getting my act together faster than my mom. "Where exactly IS my father right now, then, anyway?"

"Well," said Charlie, uncomfortably. "That's the bad news. He's sitting on a chain—and apparently has been for years— two blocks from your school, in the body of a German shepherd. I do not yet know or understand WHY he is living the life of a chained dog when the Randulf I know is powerful enough to easily remove himself from the chain and any humans who would seek to imprison him; but I suspect it has something to do with the curse he himself had the Sorceress place on our people for anyone who copulated with an Earth-dweller."

He cleared his throat, now even more ill-at-ease. "It's obvious, since Baylee has been confirmed to be the one we seek—due to the manifestation of her already-burgeoning powers—that not only did Randulf copulate with Candice, but they created life together. We can only assume this was a deliberate act on the King's part in an effort to save our people.

"This act thereby engendered the curse on the King, but as the details of said curse have been kept confidential between the King, the Sorceress, and Shanti, the Prophetess, I don't know what exactly it will take to release him. What I do know is that it won't be easy. The curse was created to be unbreakable. Our only hope is that there is some way around it that we can uncover and then unmeld the dang thing before our world and our civilization are annihilated."

He sat heavily on the floor next to Mom and myself.

Taking both of our hands in his, he looked earnestly into our eyes. "Randulf has been the best king our people have ever known. And, he's the most powerful immortal our realm has ever seen, too. Rest assured, we want him back just as much as you do; if there is some way to free him from this tortuous existence, we will succeed in doing so."

He turned to his team. "Now, who has a brilliant plan for just how we do that?"

Everyone started talking excitedly at once, happy to be given a chance to express themselves. It seemed the people of Perrin really did love King Randulf, aka, the Wrath of Dog, aka, my father after all.

I really couldn't wrap my mind around the fact that the slathering, foaming at the mouth, crazed beast I'd been skirting in fear for the last two years on my way to school was MY FATHER. *I'm gonna need a lot of therapy.*

Just how does one get over the fact that your own dad has tried to rip your head from your body, and bears supersized incisors that are tailor-made for crunching little girls who dare to walk past his territory?

Oi. Therapy may not cut it. A lobotomy sounds more promising.

Chapter 10: The Dadinator

We decided that a few of us would go back down the alley to have a discussion with Wrath of Dog *(or Randulf . . . or whatever that dog/immortal/my father's name really was)* to see if we could figure out how he got into this position and begin a formal plan for extracting him. We didn't want to drag 11 people to the area and draw attention to ourselves, just in case the cops or school officials were still combing the vicinity in search of the missing zombie cats.

Mom insisted she was going to be part of the team that went. She'd seen Wrath almost daily for the five years we lived here too; she, like me, had always pitied him, wanting to steal him and drag him into our home so he could have the normal doggy life he deserved.

But his aggression was off-putting and frankly downright scary to both of us. We weren't sure if he would ever calm down and learn to be a "real" dog if we freed him from his chain.

Or if he'd just eat us and call it a day.

I guess he was never a "real" dog to begin with.

Like me, I was sure Mom had a ton of crazy-making emotions running through her head right now, and taking action was probably the best idea so she didn't go insane with the stress. It couldn't be easy dealing with the fact that the man she loved had been here all along, trapped in the body of a dog and in a situation that was very close to hell on earth, both for actual dogs AND for him as an immortal trapped as a dog.

Charlie chose Matt and Jake—the black-haired twins—to go with me, Mom, and him on the mission, as they were the best silent ninja types on the team.

I'm down with that . . . those boys are smokin' hot. I might be half Perrinite now, whatever that meant, but I was still an almost-18-year-old girl with two eyes and a few thriving teenage hormones, after all.

It was already 9:00 p.m. when we slipped out the front door (to avoid the dog yard) and around the side of the house into the back alley. All was quiet. Maybe too quiet. The air was still, and the cold was the kind that seeped under your jacket and raised every hair as it swept along the cracks and crevasses of your body.

We slinked along the extra dark patches, hugging the edges and avoiding the street lights as much as possible; easy, given that the town saw no reason to light the areas that were not heavily traveled at night.

Probably because it's freakily creep-tastic out here. No wonder I huddled cozily in my room every night, surfing the net or playing video games with my online friends, cuddled up to BooBoo, Khronos, and maybe another cat or two.

Gah. That sounded heavenly, and I missed it already. I missed my normal life, the one that had seemed boring just yesterday.

I was sandwiched between Matt and Jake, with Charlie in the lead and Mom directly behind him. It was obvious they were trying to protect the womenfolk from unforeseen threats, which if I were a good feminist I might be bothered by; but since I was honest enough to know I'd get my bootie kicked in a fight, I appreciated their concerned attention. I had never been a big fan of the dark, and given tonight's mission, I found it extra ghoulish.

We were soon within biting range of Wrath, and I heard the familiar growl as he stalked in our direction. Like clockwork, the hairs on the back of my neck stood to attention, fear clawed its way up my esophagus, and I tried unsuccessfully to remind myself that somewhere inside that beast was my father. I shouldn't be afraid of him.

But I was.

From what I'd learned today, it was my job now, somehow, to rescue him and then lead him and his best warriors into battle to save an entire world of immortals.

Sounds doable, eh. What the hey-ell?

Charlie jerked to a stop, and the rest of us piled into him from behind. I extricated myself from the jumble of hotness in front and back of me, and moved to the right so I could see what Charlie was up to.

He had hunkered down and offered Wrath a dog treat from the pouch Mom brought with her. Ah, it was her dog-training pouch with high-value (meaning tasty) treats that somehow magically made dogs behave better because by gum they wanted that food. And they'd do anything to get it.

Good thinking, Mom, I silently applauded. *I, on the other hand, am always an hour late and three dollars short in the ideas department—or however that saying goes.*

Wrath reached out gently and took the proffered treat, at the same time catching a whiff of Charlie. This time he immediately reacted as he had earlier in the day, backing up, shaking his head, and letting loose with a long, sad whine.

I hadn't understood before when we were here, but now I got the distinct impression that the King was somehow "lost" inside Wrath, and only came to himself once he recognized Charlie as being from his home realm.

This morning after he and Charlie had scented each other, he had immediately stepped into his king role and began pondering the situation, trying to understand what was happening. It seemed that between then and now the switch had turned back off, and Randulf was left in the dark. Literally.

Well this sucks.

"I'm here now, little warrior; everything will be ok." The deep voice was back in my head. I jumped.

"Oh, I wasn't expecting to hear you in my head," I sent back via mindlink. "Since Charlie and his team took their true forms, everyone has been speaking out loud. I forgot for a second to expect you here. How are you?" I asked, concerned.

He sighed. "Just another day in feral hell for me, it would seem. Charlie, are you in here too?" he asked.

"Yes, your Highness," came the reply. I'd know Charlie's voice anywhere now; it was nowhere near as deep as the King's, but it was pleasantly cordial, even with the formality of his speech patterns. "Sir, I need to first ascertain where we stand with regard to your memory. Do you remember Candice? I've told her that you are here, and she insisted on coming with us to speak to you."

At that, we all turned toward Mom, who was quietly sobbing against the corner of the building. *Argh. I guess the stark reality had finally hit her after she got a good look at Wrath. Who could blame her.*

The King hesitated for a second, and then all but whispered in my ear. "Oh, my God. My darling!" There was so much love in that one endearment that I nearly popped a vein trying not to cry. I was definitely getting all verklempt, galldarnit.

He slowly approached her, hunkered down submissively and dragging his chain with each step. The clanking of rusted links over rock and asphalt reminded me of the predicament we faced in removing him from the curse keeping him chained here.

I didn't know how to fix this mess, and I already felt like a failure at my new job. The weight of a responsibility I didn't ask for or want hung heavy about my shoulders. I longed to toss it from my back and onto the ground like a sweaty t-shirt, but I felt it clinging, refusing to be budged.

Wrath brushed up against his newly-remembered love, gently leaning his full body weight into her. She crouched down to meet him, running her hands through his ruff, drawing him further into her. I knew he was probably filthy and smelly and hadn't had a bath in as long as 18 years, and it was a horrifying and dehumanizing thought. *De-immortalizing thought? Obviously, that didn't work. Whatevs.*

Mom wasn't fazed, though. She slowly drew back and looked him in the eye, scrutinizing, and finally seeing the answers she'd sought all these long years. It really WAS him, Randulf—her love!

In that moment she believed the unbelievable, I could see it on her face. Acceptance. Peace.

Holding his face in her hands, she continued gazing into his eyes, and whispering. "I love you, oh my sweet man, I love you so. You have no idea how long I've looked for you, how I've despaired of ever seeing you again. I have loved you these 18 long winters, pledging my heart to only you until the day I die. Now that I have you again, I will not rest until we free you and you make the journey back to me, wholly. Would that be ok with you?"

Wrath gave a short yip of joy, and slurped her right on the kisser.

Ew. I could have lived without that nasty visual for the rest of MY short life.

Mom laughed with delight, not even minding the dog slobber. *Oh, I forgot, our dogs are always doing that to her too, and she likes it; and they don't even have the excuse of a handsome king living inside their pelts.*

Mom and Randulf stayed like that for awhile, reluctant to part; she held him gently, fingers entwined in the longer fur at his ruff, and he leaned his whole body into her, letting her know as best he could that he loved and remembered her. Matt and Jake kept guard while we allowed them some privacy, one on each side of Wrath's area facing opposite directions down the alley.

So far, the coast had remained clear.

Eventually, Randulf reluctantly parted from my mom and paced back toward me. Soon, the King's voice came into my head. "Baylee, I guess by now you are aware that I am your biological father. I quickly ascertained the truth by scent when you were here this morning, but we were interrupted by the authorities and I was not able to delve into this any further with you.

"I deeply apologize that I have not been in your life for the past 18 years, and you have had to go without a father. As you can see, I've been a bit, how shall we put it, indisposed? Please know, I loved you when you were in your mother's womb, and I already love you now without yet getting the chance to know you. I can only hope you'll give me an opportunity to make things right with you once we get out of this mess."

I could no more stop the tears from flowing than I could magically blink my father back to his immortal self, so I just let them come. Those were the words I'd always yearned to hear, but long ago had resigned myself to the loss of half my heart.

Yet my father LOVED me—ME! Even if the circumstances weren't perfect, even if said father was currently a dog (a chained, smelly dog), and the words were not so much uttered but manifested into my mind, I still clung to them, and they became my undoing.

Am I not such a horrible person after all?

Charlie's voice assured me, "You were never a horrible person, of that I'm sure, young one. Now, as much as I know this reunion is long overdue, and I hate to interrupt the love-fest, we really must discuss how the King got into these dire straits and what can be done to free him. King? Can you enlighten us, please?"

Father (heck, I had no clue what to call him now . . .) began at the point where Charlie and his team had ended up in the dark. "When Shanti envisioned a female warrior who gave our world a chance of surviving the scion, I locked myself into a room with Shanti and the Sorceress, Mara, where we brainstormed for five days. This work led us to a resolution which we believed could work, but it involved a willing sacrifice from our realm."

"And that sacrifice was you, wasn't it, Sire?" asked Charlie quietly.

"Yes, it was," the King lamented, but seemingly still believing that the right choice had been made. "The warrior child had to come from the loins of one of our own, but we'd already deployed the curse for anyone who bred with a human. Since I am, or was, the strongest immortal in our dimension, it was logical that I should be the one to sacrifice myself to bring this chance to our people.

"Mara said that I'd be led to the chosen bearer, and she was right. My team of eight warriors and I came to Earth in search of a sign, learning and experiencing this dimension as it had become in the hundreds of years since I'd last been here.

"Eventually my travels led me here to Virginia, and the moment I laid eyes on Candice, even as she lay face down on the asphalt along the Appalachian Trail, I felt a certain pull and an inner knowing that I had found my mate.

"So I rescued her, nurtured her, and fell in love, for the very first time in my life. Every second with her proved more delightful than the last, and I couldn't get enough of this woman, these heavenly sensations rampaging through my system. My God! I finally understood why our people had so blatantly disregarded Perrin's instructions on breeding and copulating with humans all those centuries ago. I was so in love that I allowed myself to believe the two of us could break the curse, could have our happily ever after.

"My team warned me otherwise, and begged me not to get too attached, but really, what would it have mattered? The curse didn't fall solely on those who knew love. Anyone who copulated with a human would fall victim. So I held off from the final act as long as I could. When we finally made love . . ."

"Hold on," I inserted, holding my hand up to stave off further disclosures. "TMI. I don't want to hear about my parents copulating, ew! Let's just say kissed from now on, that's about as much as my sensitive teenage stomach can handle."

Father chuckled. "Ok, daughter, we finally kissed. And made a baby. The end. But strangely, I was not immediately afflicted with the curse, and I didn't know why. I wasn't complaining, though. This allowed me to stay with your mother and you, growing in her tummy, through most of her pregnancy. It was the most joyous period of my long life, and I tried to etch each moment into my memory for when the time came that I would be ripped from you both."

He seemed to be struggling with his own overwhelming emotions now. "And then the day finally arrived."

CHAPTER 11: WHAT NOW

I wanted to hear more—every single morsel, in fact—but at that moment a police cruiser turned into the alleyway. When he saw the five of us standing around a chained dog, he hit his lights and zoomed toward us, eager to catch us in some kind of illegal tomfoolery.

Uh oh. This was all Mom needed, another run-in with the local police. Over a dog, no less.

They'd be sure to think she was stealing Wrath, and she couldn't afford another arrest, given that she was still working the legal system for the last chained dog she'd helped.

Wrath must have read her mind, because he whined and nuzzled her hand with his snout. He seemed to be telling her it would be ok, and maybe sending some of his special mindgrind juice her way.

She relaxed, and the calm was catchy, because suddenly I felt better too.

"Hey, cut it out, Dad!" I protested. "I mean, keep Mom mellow, but count me out. I need my wits about me."

I could feel the wave of tranquility ease off, and for that I was grateful. I needed to be able to deal with this officer, and I couldn't let my mind be all fuddled up with Gandhi crap.

Just as the officer reached us, I asked Dad (sigh, was

I calling him Dad now? I was so confused!) if he'd do the mindgrind on him. "Of course I could," he replied, "but I don't think I'll need to. Charlie is just as competent as me, and I have a feeling he can handle about anything that comes his way."

No sooner had he said that than the policeman turned off his lights and continued down the alleyway, as if he'd completely forgotten we existed. He probably had, with a little help.

Saweet! Works for me.

Charlie came back online with Wrath and me. "I don't think he'll be back the rest of the evening. I sent him to get donuts for the whole precinct, and to stay at the station guarding them until they have all been devoured, Your Highness," his smile of genuine amusement at his own shenanigans tugged at my heartstrings.

I think I want to adopt him as my gay uncle.

He rolled his eyes, but kept talking. "So, Sir, where were we? Why and how did you disappear from Candice and Baylee's lives?"

My father gave a heavy sigh and shook his head. "That's a long story, but I guess we have time. Baylee, can you relay what I'm saying to your mom so she is not kept in the dark? And Charlie, feel free to keep your team apprised via mindlink while we talk."

He continued. "I'll tell you everything I know, but as you'll see, there are gaps in my memory. Basically, the curse was set up to turn any guilty parties into their animal forms, permanently . . . only now they would be feral in addition. So not only would they NOT remember their immortality, but they would also completely forget their life on Perrin as an immortal living in human form.

"In other words, they were destined to spend all of eternity here on earth as an animal in the wild.

"Since we created the curse, we've had five Perrin citizens betray it, and they, to my knowledge, are still living on earth in animal form. I don't know or understand why I didn't transform immediately after copulating with Candice—I'm incredibly grateful for the additional time we had together, but it doesn't make sense to me.

"What I do know, however, is that when I turned, the rest of my team of elite warriors also transformed into their animal forms and went feral. That hasn't happened with anyone else, either, and I feel responsible for what befell these innocent men and women. I need to fix it. And them."

He paused here for a moment, while I updated Mom on everything he'd relayed so far. Watching her face go through so much agony as I explained what had happened to the man she loved made me want to reach out and hold her. I wasn't used to seeing her so vulnerable. I rubbed her arm through her thick winter jacket.

Wrath continued. "But here's where things get tricky. When we first turned feral, we lived out in the mountains near the Appalachian Trail as a pack of wild dogs. As Charlie knows, all nine of us are highly trained fighters, both in our canine forms and in our human forms. But something happened to us out there, and we were overpowered. I just don't know how or by whom. My memory of what happened is fuzzy because, due to the curse, I was nothing more than a beast at the time. I have a shadowy picture in my mind of being surrounded by men in black ninja gear. I believe we were shot with dart guns and then I blacked out."

The regal shepherd turned and faced the alley, deep in thought. While he tried to pull the reluctant memories from his mind, I took the opportunity to again update Mom. She walked over and absently ran her fingers through his thick ruff while I talked. I assumed Charlie was updating Matt and Jake through their mindlink connections, because they nodded in acknowledgement a couple of times, but otherwise betrayed no emotion. They were good.

I'm gonna need to find out more about this mindlink, and what I can use it for. And if I can make it more reliable, too.

So far I seemed to solely be able to hear Charlie and Wrath, and only when they allowed me to. I didn't like that they seemed to always be in my head, but could keep me out of theirs whenever they wanted. I needed that skillset.

"All my memories for the last 18 years have been as a feral before you two got through to me this morning, so I'm having a hard time making sense of them with any kind of logic. When I woke up, I was in some kind of facility, and they were affixing this chain to me. I remember that it was incredibly painful, and I was howling in agony. My pack members returned my howls, so at that time they were still in the facility with me."

He seemed incredibly forlorn. I imagined it must be very difficult to live as a pack and have that taken from you. He'd been so alone and in such awful conditions for so long now.

"After that I never saw or heard a single member of my pack again. There was some kind of mindblind blocking being used in that facility, or we were kept drugged, because we could not communicate as we had in the woods. I couldn't reach their minds, even though I knew from their howls that they were there. Somewhere.

"I've been taken to a few different locations throughout the years, but I believe I've been in this location for a long while. I'm not a good judge of time in my feral form. I have always been chained since my capture, and I haven't had a bath, a swim, or a run in all the time I've been held captive."

My heart broke for him in that moment. I just couldn't imagine this kind of torment to any animal or living being, let alone a dog who was essentially wild and needed to be able to flee, to fight, or to take cover when he felt threatened. He could do nothing a normal dog could do, and he was stuck in a feral's mind at that. What a horrible mess.

"The weirdest thing is," he said, "I can't shake the feeling that I'm here to guard something—but I don't know what it is. There's a black cloud over my awareness when I try to recall anything having to do with it—like I'm not supposed to be able to remember it."

He finished. "Lastly, I believe these chains are more than just chains, like they themselves are some kind of mindlink. I suspect I am monitored somehow through them or an implant in my body that I don't know about. Which makes me think you all should take your leave for tonight. I don't want to risk them finding us together, and I believe they come to this house late at night. Tomorrow is a new day, and maybe if you all pool your brain matter resources and given this new information you can figure out how to rescue me."

Then he made a plea that literally ripped my heart in two. "Could I please have some water tomorrow? I long for nothing more than fresh, clean water. I usually have to drink from puddles, and sometimes I go without food or water at all for days. Because I'm immortal I survive where a regular dog might die, but it's still very painful to endure. And, some high-quality food would be much appreciated, too. Thank you, Daughter, Charles. Thank you for finding me and for not leaving me here to die. Please tell Candice I love her still these many years later....And, that she's just as beautiful as the day I met her."

I'll admit it, I caved to my inner child. This was my father enduring these conditions, conditions that no living being should have to tolerate for even a second. Maybe it was everything that had happened today, or maybe it was his heartwrenching appeal, but soon big old globby chunks of snot were rolling out my nose, and rivulets of water were streaming from the corners of my eyes.

I didn't have any tissues, either, so the sleeves of my coat had to bear the brunt of the goop.

Ugh. I hoped tomorrow would be a better day.

Mom gave Wrath a big hug goodbye while he again leaned into her to show his affection in the only way possible. Then we slowly made our way home, our grief over his circumstances tempered with joy that he was actually alive and worry over how we were going to free him. In addition, we had to uncover who had captured him, what they were guarding, and where the rest of his warriors were being held. We had a lot on our plates.

Mom got everyone squared away with places to sleep— *Thank Dog she was here for logistical issues since I was clueless*—and I gratefully took Khronos and BooBoo upstairs with me to crawl into bed for snuggles. My cozy bed in my familiar room was without a doubt where I felt the safest, and I needed that security tonight.

I was asleep before I even managed to pull off my clothes and switch them for jammies.

Chapter 12: Experiment

Saturday morning brought with it a weariness that quickly dissipated once the fog around my brain lifted. I wasn't excited to be—whatever THIS was I was supposed to be—but I wanted to, no, needed to, free my father.

If that meant that I must be different than I always thought I was or would grow to be, I would embrace that change. I was even a little excited about it, truth be told.

Freeing Wrath had become my number one goal in life right now. Not only for myself—even though I eagerly sought the chance to know my father and feel loved by him. What kid wouldn't?

I mean, the fact that my missing and presumed dead father had come back into my life was like a Hallmark movie come true—if said Hallmark movie came with chained feral dogs and talking zombie cats, of course.

I actually had a father now. How cool was that?

But beyond that, beyond what I wanted and wanted to believe I deserved, I had seen the look on my mother's face last night. There had been so much longing, so much love, and so much hope when she looked into Wrath's eyes that I had to make her dream come true. Had to.

Apparently I'm the 'chosen' one with some kind of latent

ability to get things done, so let's get to it.

I jumped out of bed. *Dad's not gonna rescue himself, or he'd have done it 18 years ago.*

I rushed downstairs where I found the team already up and whipping up a big breakfast in the kitchen. Mom's eyes sparkled, and she laughed and joked with Charlie and the others as she created a monstrous fruit salad and instructed her helpers in the toast, fried potatoes, and pancakes department. I'd never seen her so happy, and it gave me a lift.

I started to whip up a big batch of egg substitute—we used The Vegg which was trés delicious—so I stepped back and did the calculations to make sure I had enough for everyone. I also dug out the blender for this massive undertaking, because I wanted to be sure my end of the deal was extra smooth and tasty to stack up to such a delicious breakfast.

We'd become mostly vegan now, eschewing even dairy and eggs at home, but we tried not to freak out on the rare occasions when we dined out. We didn't want to monitor every crumb that went into our mouths or grill waitstaff about every ingredient, so when we ate at a restaurant or a friend's home, we probably ended up ingesting eggs and/or dairy and tried not to stress too hard about it.

Our "no meat" rule always stayed firm, however, no matter where we were.

I have to admit, it was nice that Mom and I both agreed to this lifestyle. It made cooking and eating together so much more pleasant than it would be if we ate two different meals at every sitting.

She hadn't forced me to espouse the idea of vegetarianism, but after I'd done some research on my own and watched a few movies about the horrific lives they lead on factory farms, I got onboard with the idea.

I loved animals as much as she did, and I didn't see any reason to eat them if there was any way around it. As it turned out, it was much easier than I expected it to be. In today's grocery stores, there are so many delicious and excellent substitutions available that we were always trying out new things, and had even taken up a lively "new recipe" mother-daughter cooking event once a week.

Sometimes the food didn't turn out like the recipe pictured—once in awhile it was even less than edible—but we got a good laugh out of it, bonded over it, and it became our thing. Together, we had made the decision to lean vegan as much as possible after a year as vegetarians. It worked for us.

Even if the gang had no intention of becoming vegan (I didn't yet have a good handle on what they ate in Perrin or how it compared), they listened intently to everything we said and did, soaking up the knowledge like little education-deprived sponges. While they stayed in our home we'd be eating as a group, so they were content to help with the cooking and wanted to understand how to do it themselves so they wouldn't be a burden on us.

It turned out that Bradley and Tara—brown tabby and white long-hair in their cat forms, I reminded myself, trying to keep them all straight—were the chefs of the bunch. While everyone was competent in the kitchen because on Perrin everyone carried their share of the workload, Bradley and Tara showed an amazing knack for spices and cooking. Tara explained that cooking to her was scientific in nature due to the precise measurements and chemical reactions between ingredients, which made it fascinating to experiment with.

Bradley was the foodie of the group, however, and loved to eat an array of foods at each meal; he got grumpy if he was forced to eat the same things all the time, and I was informed was prone to becoming hangry if he went too long between meals.

Duly noted.

He was super-excited about the food on earth because it was so different from theirs. He asked questions non-stop, even digging out Mom's cookbook so he could figure out how to spice the potatoes just right so they went with The Vegg but still provided a unique flavor.

They were a rowdy bunch, talking and laughing together as they cooked. It was obvious they'd been a team for a long, long time, and relentlessly teased each other but in a way that brought laughter and not pain. I could tell Mom loved it too, and we both had smiles plastered on our faces. It felt like we were eating with Dad's extended family who we'd known forever, even though we'd just met them yesterday.

Dad! Ugh. We've gotta take him food and water ASAP.

I lost my appetite then, picturing my father out there with no food or water. Luckily I had eaten my fill already, so I put my leftovers and some of the potatoes and pancakes in a separate container.

"Hey, guys," I said, loudly so as to be heard over the din of their breakfast conviviality. "I'm going to run this food and fresh water up to Wrath. I can't stand to think of him suffering out there even one minute longer. I'll be right back."

Charlie stood. "I'm coming with you, young warrior. You should not yet be alone with him, as we don't know if you can get past his feral mind on your own. Then, when we return, we shall immediately get started on your evaluation so we can make progress toward freeing the King and getting the curse removed."

He instructed his team to help Mom with cleanup, and had Matt and Jake lead a brainstorming session while we were gone, as they knew everything my father had said last night. Any and all ideas were to be written down so we could discuss them as a team later and move forward with a plan.

I felt so relieved not to be carrying this heavy load by myself. Charlie was such a competent team leader, and a remarkable person, that I felt safe when he was nearby. I would have had no idea how to grow into my talents and use them to free Wrath on my own, but now that burden was not sitting squarely and solely on my scrawny shoulders. I had eleven people, including Mom, backing me up and playing on my team.

Whew.

Wrath was in a foul mood this morning, and immediately raised both his hackles and mine as we approached. *Argh, I'm never going to get over my fear of him as a dog! This does not bode well for our future father-daughter relationship.*

But as soon as we got within scenting distance and he was able to smell Charlie, he calmed down, shook his head, whined, and then backed off his aggressive stance.

I waited for him to greet me before moving forward those last few steps, wanting to be sure he was safely HIM again.

"Good morning, daughter. I'm happy to see your face this morning, despite the harsh greeting I probably gave you whilst in my feral state. You look like you had a good night's sleep. Are you rested and ready to begin your training today?"

"Yes, but I'm nervous, to be honest. Yesterday I had no idea I wasn't a normal, everyday American teenager. Now today I'm half Perrinite, and supposed to have super-powers and save a world I've never seen from destruction. But inside I still feel like I'm just me."

He rubbed against me in sympathy.

"I know it's difficult, but I also know you'll succeed. There's simply too much at stake for failure, and you have all of us to help you move forward. Well, as soon as we figure out a way to remove these chains and this feral fog from my mind, that is. I'm afraid I'm not much use to you until we do."

I gave him the food and water I'd brought, and watched in tears as he ripped into the food like he hadn't eaten in a week. I vowed to feed him twice a day until we got him out of this dilemma. It was heartbreaking watching the suffering he had endured for the last 18 years and knowing we could never undo what had been done to him.

But by who?

Maybe it was actually a blessing that he'd had a feral mind through most of it.

Charlie cleared his throat. "Have you been able to remember anything else since last evening, Your Highness?

"Unfortunately not, Charles. You'd only been gone a few minutes when the madness again descended upon me. I simply cannot fight it without your mental strength to pull from. Which reminds me—every time I've successfully come back to myself, both you and Baylee have been in my presence together. I know that in the end it is my memory of your scent, Charles, that clicks for me, but can I pull myself out without Baylee here? I'd like to try that as a first experiment."

Charlie and I agreed we'd walk in the direction of school, and then he'd come back by himself in five minutes time. Since he could easily mindlink with me from that short distance, I could run to his aid if things got hairy.

The school looked normal for a Saturday. There was no one around; no staff, no cops, no students. That was good; maybe yesterday's brouhaha had passed with relatively little fanfare.

I should get online and see what the local paper's Facebook page says. Or, call Amaya, the original town crier.

While Charlie walked back to see if he could get through to Wrath, I called Amaya. She picked up on the first ring.

"OMFG, girl!" she shrieked. "Where in fifty-shades-of-pumpernickel have you been? I've texted you like a million times since yesterday, and you responded only ONCE. ONCE! Why are you blowing me off? Did you hear about the zombie cats? I don't ever want to step foot in that school again!"

God, I missed that girl. She made me feel happy and irritated all at the same time; it was her gift. As usual, she was running her motor mouth and asking five trillion questions without leaving a single space between them for me to actually answer her.

"Calm down, wench," I laughed. "I had family come in from out of town unexpectedly, so I've been swamped with dealing with them and just got away for a few minutes to call you."

"Family? What family? You never told me about any relatives. Your mom was an only child! What's going on here?" She sounded suspicious.

Oh, for the love of black raspberries. What? Raspberries rock! *Especially the ones you pick yourself in the woods. Yum.*

I really should stop holding discussions with myself.

If Amaya didn't believe me, I'd be in for a world a' hurtin'. She was totally the detective type. Once she got a whiff of something fishy, she never backed off until she got all the dirt.

I'm gonna have to up my acting skills. I need a class, obviously. Acting 101 for Introverts.

"These guys are on my father's side, I never met them before. They called yesterday when they came into town and asked if they could come over and meet Mom and I. So we've been hanging out with them ever since. They're pretty cool."

She still seemed dubious. "Well, do I get to meet them? How long are they staying? Does this mean we can't go to the movies tonight like we planned? You promised we'd go see the new Ryan Gosling movie! You know I need a pretty boy fix."

I agreed with her there. What's not to love about Ryan Gosling? Yeah, he was starting to get a little old for us, but he was still super sexy and droolworthy.

And, *The Notebook.* 'Nuf said.

"Ugh, I don't know if I can get away. Mom said something about going out to dinner. I'll text you later and let you know. I'm sorry!" I hated lying to her, but I wasn't in a position yet to tell her the truth. So fudging was the best I could do.

She pouted. "I don't want to call any of those other lame-o's we sometimes hang with, but I guess I'll have to. I can't miss this movie. Let me know ASAP if you can meet up. Love you! But I'm still mad. Just in case you didn't realize. Bye."

"Baylee, HELP!" The strangled cry came pounding into my brain. *Oh, hell.* I turned and sprinted the two blocks to Wrath's yard, hoping Charlie could hold on until I arrived.

I should have been paying more attention. And I'm breathless . . . need . . . to work out. . . more.

Charlie was on the ground while Wrath loomed over him, growling and foaming at the mouth. *Great, Dad's rabid.* Just then Wrath sunk his teeth into Charlie's arm, and a loud and decidedly unmanly shriek erupted from Charlie's mouth. *Double doody.*

Why wasn't Wrath coming around?

I rushed up to the dog, and, without thinking, ripped him off Charlie, launching him ten feet into the air. He landed hard and with a deep oomph.

Argh, now I killed my father. Not my week. How did I suddenly turn into Wonder Woman?

I had thrown Denise the bully earlier in the week, and now that action suddenly made more sense to me. I'd assumed it was just an adrenaline rush, but apparently it'd been my powers manifesting all along.

Well, she deserved that and more.

I hurried over to Charlie where he lay rolling and moaning on the ground, "Charlie, Charlie. Are you ok?"

"The experiment was informative," he said wryly. "We now know that Wrath doesn't recognize me without you present. Are you excited to try it the other way around?"

"Um . . . no?" I retorted, terrified. "I've been having to get by this dog for years, and he always tries to rip my head off. I don't see why it would be any different today. But, I guess one more time won't kill me. I hope."

He chuckled, giving me his good arm to help him up.

Wrath slowly pulled himself off the ground and limped over to us. "I'm sorry, Father," I started. "I didn't mean to throw you that far. I was just afraid for Charlie. Apparently one of my skills is manifesting, and I don't know my own strength."

His deep voice was weaker than usual. "It is I who am sorry. Charles, I didn't know you without Baylee present. I thought you were the key to overcoming my feral side, but nothing clicked for me this time. Is your arm ok?"

Charlie nodded. "I can feel my massive muscles pushing the rabies right out, Your Highness," he joked.

"Har, har, har," I said, relieved that the worst of it was over, and that Charlie apparently had accelerated healing. I hoped I was destined to get that too! That would be one awesome gift to have.

The King chuffed out a short bark of laughter, and we decided to repeat the experiment, only with me this time. Charlie waited the two blocks away at the school; as I walked hesitantly down the alley, I couldn't help but feel like I was walking to my own demise.

Obviously, I'm suffering from chained dog attack PTSD. Should I get therapy now or wait until I save the world, I mused.

Better wait. I have a feeling there's a lot more where that came from.

I approached Wrath cautiously, not stupid enough to get too close like Charlie had. This time he sat back, resting upright on his haunches and waited, watching me. I felt creeped out by his stare, but he didn't seem to be acting aggressively, so I told myself everything would be ok.

"Dad?" I asked. "Are you in there?" I crept a little nearer, and just as I did he launched himself at me from his crouched position, landing directly on top of me, toppling me backward.

"Argh!" I screamed. "Charlie!"

I was the one down for the count this time, barely holding Wrath's head away from my body and trying to avoid his snapping jaws. Charlie must have used his flash ability, which I'd heard about but hadn't yet seen, because in the next instant he was grabbing Wrath by the tail and yanking him off me.

I was never so relieved to see that English-speaking mug in my life.

Wrath immediately came to his senses, and sat back heavily.

"Well," he said. "Now we have our answer. There is something about the two of you together that pulls me out of my feral mind, but only the two of you combined, and only when you're both within range of me. This complicates things."

He lay down despondently on the ground in front of us. "Baylee, you know I would never intentionally hurt you. My feral mind just doesn't know any better, and sees you, or anyone, as a threat. Since I am on this chain, I have only two instincts, fight or flight. As fleeing is impossible for me, I choose to fight, each and every time. I am so sorry, Young One. I know that I am causing you mental anguish, and it's the last thing as a father I should be doing. My deepest apologies, to both you and Charles."

I was still shaken up, but tried to hide my level of despair and fear. He could probably smell it on me. "That's ok, Father. I know you aren't intending to harm us, but I'm glad we now know what we are up against. Charlie, let's go brainstorm with the others to work out a plan to get Dad free."

We said our goodbyes, promised to come back later in the evening with more food and any ideas we'd come up with, and made our way slowly down the alley.

Wrath watched us forlornly, howling his frustration and loneliness, and tugging my heartstrings right from my body. It was not a good morning.

Chapter 13: Ninja-mode

We dragged ourselves back inside to find the team in fight mode. They'd split up into pairs and were working their best ninja drills, thrilled to be out of feline form and back in human—or immortal, whatever—mode, but feeling a need to work out the kinks. They'd cleared the living room, pushing the furniture to the sides, and shut the dogs out into the yard for their safety while they trained.

Mom was upstairs deep into her monthly cat room cleaning, so Charlie teamed up with me to find out what I was capable of.

I didn't have high hopes about my abilities. So far we'd discovered that I had some super strength, at least in confrontational situations, and I could do the mindlink with both Charlie and Randulf.

I was gonna need more than that to save the world, I was pretty sure.

Charlie came at me for the third time, while I stood there in a daze. *Focus, Bay!* I moved to the side at the last second, and, for once, sidestepped the surprise assault he'd aimed my way. He simply nodded his approval and came at me again.

Well, so much for encouragement.

I spent more time on the floor than on my feet, and my

bruises begat baby bruises they were multiplying so quickly. We were focusing on combining my mindlink with my strength triggers, but I was feeling incredibly frustrated. Nothing seemed to really get me past what we'd already seen, and neither Charlie nor I knew where to turn from here.

Daniel stopped what he was doing and watched us for a moment. He waggled his eyebrows at me, and took off upstairs. He was back in a flash (I so needed to learn how to do that!) with BooBoo in his hands, and making a motion like he was going to break his neck.

What!? Nobody touches BooBoo kitty! Somewhere inside me I had an inkling that he was deliberately provoking me to see what he could trigger, but I was pretty touchy about protecting our animals, especially BooBoo. I felt the heat start at my toes and rise on up, with the energy again expanding outward from my spine.

I launched myself off the floor and was on him in a flash. *How in combat boot heaven did I do that?!* I had felt a primal urge to save my baby, and I don't think my feet even moved.

I just projected myself the way Charlie and most of his team can do! I was elated, but the thought didn't slow me down; it was like my brain was split into two and I could focus on so much more at any given moment.

I grabbed Daniel by the throat, wrested my baby from his grasp, and handed him off to Charlie for protection. Daniel allowed me to easily take him away, wearing a big cheesy grin on his face like he'd somehow won the prize.

I'll show you prize, I fumed. I kicked his legs out from under him and took him down, hard, as a lesson not to touch my cat again. EVER.

I think he got the message.

He slowly rolled onto his side, looking at Charlie, and said "I think she might be a little stronger than the rest of us, Boss. I feel like my guts are gonna spill out all over the floor." He cradled his stomach like he was holding himself together, and Tara rushed over to him, feeling him up and down to make sure nothing was broken. Or oozing out onto the throw rug. *Ugh.*

Tara, being the scientist of the bunch, had spent years studying medicine, and acted as the team doctor anytime their accelerated healing wasn't kicking in as expected. She was great with herbs and natural healing remedies when needed, too.

Now I just feel ashamed. My adrenalin had worn off, and I better understood that Daniel was merely trying to evoke the intense feelings necessary for me to reach my powers. Theoretically, the team explained to me, the more my strengths were triggered through heightened emotions, the more familiar I'd become with reaching for them, and the easier it would be for me to access them on demand.

I moved to his other side. "I'm so sorry, Daniel. I just saw red when you came downstairs holding BooBoo. Even though a tiny part of me knew you weren't really going to kill him, I couldn't stop myself from attacking you. Can you forgive me?"

He ran his hands through his red hair and pretended to be deep in thought. "I guess so, this one time," he teased, feigning reluctance. "But I'll think twice about pissing you off again, that's for sure." His words took a more serious note.

"Boss, this might be a good thing," he addressed Charlie again. "If the enemy underestimates her the way I just did, she may have the element of surprise on her side."

Rebecca and Ruth, the Asian twins with the multi-hued and multi-layered locks, looked me up and down and then stepped forward. "We'd like to spend a little time training her, if you all don't mind," said Rebecca. "We have some ideas that might help her open up to and access her powers more freely. We need to be alone though, or at least in the company of females only. We'll need to be able to take a look at her energy system without her attire getting in the way."

Well, that sounds hella awkward.

The guys shrugged, seemingly unembarrassed; they all spent so much time nude around each other when they came out of the change that they took it in stride. They got, however, that it was downright horrifying for me, so Charlie integrated with the other males and they continued to train downstairs while I worked upstairs with the ladies.

Rebecca, Ruth, Tara, and I trudged up the steps to do the dirty deed, aka, get me into my birthday suit. *I didn't sign up for this, dagnabit.*

Rebecca explained that they could see auras, but the clothes on earth these days were so synthetic that they were interfering with the "signal." "So if you disrobe, we'll be able to see what your energy is doing when it unfurls, and help you learn how to guide it into the areas you need to."

Well, here goes nothing. I nervously peeled away the layers, taking a minute to confirm that I really had to go all the way to, well, you know.

Yes, yes I did.

When I was in the buff and looking around the room at anything but the ladies—ill at ease would have been an extreme understatement for how I was feeling—Ruth spoke up for the first time. "Ok, now Baylee, can you please try to access the energy you felt downstairs when Daniel made you so angry and afraid? We need to see what energy is at play in your aura and how to help you embrace it."

I tried to forget about my state of undress, and focus on pulling the by-now-familiar feeling up from my toes. I reached out for the memory of it starting at my feet and working its way up my body, exploding when it hit my abdomen and back area.

I felt a faint trickle, and expanded my consciousness into the thin weave of energy in order to force more mojo into it. I was elated when it responded to me without a trigger for the first time. I felt it travel up my legs and hit my spine, and then a massive whoosh rushed to my head. I was so shocked and dizzy that I almost fell over backwards, but Tara grabbed my arm and steadied me.

All three ladies drew in a surprised breath. They stared at my abdomen with wide eyes, so I looked down too, just in time to witness a yellow light burst from my solar plexus, encircle my body, and connect back up with itself.

Ruth exclaimed "I'm never seen such a powerful energy field, especially in one so young. That would make sense, though," she mumbled, like she was talking to herself. *Which I can relate to.* "If she's to be the savior of our people, she needs to have a strong bond with herself, and faith in her own ability to make a difference in the world."

She thought for a moment longer, working through her plan. "Baylee, stand still, ok? This will feel strange, but rest assured that I'm a skilled energy worker. I'm going to reach my hands into this third chakra energy we are seeing, and manipulate it just a tad to ensure it connects up with the two chakras below it, which are open and attempting to meld. It will not harm you, but may feel a little uncomfortable, like when you have an itch but scratching won't make it go away."

I steeled myself for the weirdness coming my way. *I might as well go join a damn Ashram*, I grumbled to myself. Ruth came closer, and her hands started weaving their way through the yellow energy field. I giggled. *It tickles!*

She messed with my aura for a few minutes, and was finally satisfied with the results of her tinkering. Suddenly her voice filled my brain. "There, I think that should do it. Let's see if this changes things."

"Um, you're in my head now, Ruth," I said out loud so that everyone could hear. She looked startled, and quickly cut me off from her thoughts, but not before I felt a wave of sheer panic wash through her mind. *Interesting.* I could feel it when she blocked me, like she put up an instant wall.

I so need to learn how to do that.

Rebecca nodded her approval. "Great! Focus on me and then Tara, or both of us at once if possible, and see if you can link with us too."

I tried them one at a time, and then together, and was able to link up both ways, although I found handling multiple people a struggle. I didn't feel overburdened with Charlie and Randulf, but I guessed that was because they were among the strongest immortals on Perrin. Rebecca explained that I'd get better at it . . . it was like building a muscle, and the more I practiced the better I'd become.

Tara was pleased with our progress. "I believe, if you're as strong as we think you are, each of your remaining four chakras will open over time, allowing access to greater and stronger abilities. For now, we'll work with what we have, and keep expanding your capacities as we go. How are you feeling right now?" she asked, looking a little concerned.

I tried for humor. "Um, naked and afraid?" I said, and chortled. *Maybe I'm becoming drunk with my new-found powers.* They'd never heard of the TV show, since they'd spent the last year as cats and the few hundred years before that on another dimension, so I had to explain the premise to them while I was getting dressed, promising we'd google it later.

I was so dog-tired from the physical exertion of learning to dodge and fight and the mental exertion of accessing my psychic energies, that everyone agreed I'd earned an hour-long nap.

Being the savior sucks. Jesus can have that all to himself.

I'll just ponder my Buddha-like wisdom from under my covers for a minute. I snickered at my own comic genius, right up until the second I fell fast asleep.

CHAPTER 14: MINDLINK

I opened my eyes, memories of the day's training flooding in; those thoughts, combined with the sore muscles and bruises that made every movement brutal, convinced me I was gonna have to quit this job I'd signed up for without my knowledge.

Seriously. *WTF. Who does these things?*

It was super quiet in the house, so I slogged my way to the cat room to get a little purr-fect lovin'. I missed my babies! I felt like I hadn't had a second to myself OR to spend with the animals since I left for school yesterday morning.

It was insane how much had happened since then. I knew the pace of my life couldn't continue so frenetically; I had no idea why the house was so hushed right now, but I had no immediate plans to find out.

Mom had the room as close to spotless as it gets; I loved the monthly cleaning days, because everything sparkled. Don't get me wrong, I kept a handle on most things during the week and she usually gave a light cleaning every Saturday too, but once a month she went more in-depth, and that kept the room looking its best.

The cats were excited to see me and wrapped themselves around my legs, each looking for his or her scoop of kitty attention. I loved all our cats, but if I'm being honest there's always that one or two that dig themselves deeper into your heart.

Tootie, a semi-feral black tuxedo kitty who was overly fond of kibble and dragged her belly along like an extra appendage, was my second love. She was trapped by another rescuer and was discovered to be a bit more tame than the others in the litter.

The vet thought she was pregnant, so we reluctantly took her in, only to discover three months down the road that there were no babies. We got her spayed and kept her here with us because by then she'd become attached to me, and we couldn't bear to put her through the stress of another home—if one could even be found for a cat like her. I was equally as attached to her and her tubby white belly anyway, so no one had to convince me she needed to stay.

She'd hop up on my lap, lean herself into me, and rub her little face all over mine, purring all the while. Then, at the first sign of trouble (or even an unfamiliar sound), she'd be off like a shot and crammed into one of her little hidey holes.

Una was my other baby, his gray fur soft and his temperament the most doglike. He was Ishy-Squishy and the cuddliest of them all. He followed me everywhere, talking loudly and demanding his daily brushings. I think he thought he was a person.

I sat in my favorite spot for kitty snuggles, in the corner near the door, and they piled on top of me. As I absentmindedly caressed and kissed their little munchkin faces, I thought about what powers I'd manifested so far. I knew I had to get serious about this, not only to save my father from his horrendous life, but also to figure out who was behind the kidnapping of his team, what they were using the ferals for, and how that pertained to the coming apocalypse on Perrin.

I had begun to manifest super-strength the day I threw Denise, the school bully, but hadn't realized it at the time. I'd also used this same power when I'd wrested Wrath off Charlie, and when I'd "punished" Daniel for threatening to hurt BooBoo.

Although I wasn't yet accessing that strength without a dire need, hopefully the ability would be tappable when it was most crucial. I could also mindlink with both Charlie and Wrath, and even accessed the three female team members today, so theoretically I could link with all the team members if I tried.

I had flashed myself to Daniel's side when he targeted BooBoo, and even though I have no idea how I did it or how to do it again, that upgrade must be currently in my bag of tricks now too.

Not too shabby.

Rebecca believed that as my remaining chakras opened, more powers would manifest with each stage; so I should have faith that there was more to come. I would need much more to fight the burgeoning war, that much was certain.

Tara also told me that my energy field was stronger than any she'd seen on Perrin, so hopefully the universe was providing me the tools I needed to get the job done.

After I got my kitty lovins' fix out of the way, and I was feeling a tad bit more serene about the whole scenario, I moseyed downstairs to see where everyone was. I discovered that Mom and Charlie were engrossed in low-pitched and muffled discussions in her office. *I wonder what that's about? Probably swapping stories about my father.* I didn't intrude.

Daniel had set the team on a round-the-clock watch schedule, so he was taking his turn checking the fenceline and making sure all was as it should be. The team hadn't yet observed any true cause for alarm, but wanted to take precautions in case we'd missed anything or we'd been caught on camera when we met with Wrath. I realized they were thinking smarter than I, since none of those elements of warfare had even dawned on me. I had a lot to learn.

Rebecca, Ruth, Smith, Bradley, and Tara had walked the three blocks to the nearest grocery store, as Bradley and Tara were planning a vegan gourmet dinner for everyone tonight.

Now THAT's something to get excited about!

I breathed a sigh of relief that I was off the hook for dinner duty. One day of that responsibility for a team this size had been enough to last me. Conceivably, Bradley and Tara would continue their menu experimentation in the upcoming days, or as long as they stuck around. The other three had gone along to explore the bazillion food choices at Earthen grocery stores, and to pick out some new junk foods to taste. I assumed they were also on tap to schlep bags back from the store.

Matt and Jake, the twins who I'd been lucky enough to be sandwiched between on the way to Wrath's last night (they *were* on the delicious side), had made themselves comfy on the couch, and were watching one of the action dramas offered up on Netflix.

Mom must have helped them figure out the TV setup, unless the male remote-control gene crosses all dimensions. I stifled a laugh. They both smiled, waved me over, and gestured for me to sit between them. *Don't mind if I do.*

Matt's teasing voice sounded in my head. "Before you

get too dirty with your super-lusty musings about us, you should know that we can hear your thoughts now. We've got the connection open. So, you really think we're delicious, then, do you?" He grinned mischievously, pulling me down between them.

My face burned, and I wanted to crawl under the nearest furniture item and pretend they couldn't see or hear me. Now I was paranoid about thinking anything at all, so I was trying to blank my mind, not allow my abject horror to be read by them.

Next it was Jake's turn to tease, but I couldn't tell their voices apart, even in my head. "Don't worry, sweetie. Matt's being a buttmunch. We'll train you how to block us out so you can think all the dirty little thoughts you want about us. Well, me anyway. Matt's head's already too big, he doesn't need any more girls looking his way."

Matt reached over me and punched Jake in the arm. That was all it took for a full-on brother-skirmish to begin, and they rolled off the couch, wrestling and calling each other weird, made-up pet names. *It's really kinda cute.*

"We heard that," echoed in my mind, both brothers projecting at once.

"Ok, that's IT," I said, done with the embarrassment. Time for a change. "Stop goofing around and get up here and help me learn to block you guys out. I need my thoughts to be my own, dammit! Yes, I'll probably think more teenage-girl licentiousness about you both in the near future—and probably other manly men too—but that's my own beeswax. Help me, please?" Admittedly, I'd started out strong; however, I was all but whining now.

"Fine, fine," Matt pouted. "For the record, I like hearing

your naughty little nuggets. But whatever—it's really very simple, and I can't believe no one else taught you yet. Focus on me for a second. Can you feel a connection between my mind and yours? That's why we call it a mindlink after all. You can actually feel us linking up."

I stood very still, and focused all my attention on finding the bond he spoke of. I was getting better at identifying when my energy was being used to mindlink, and I finally "saw" the connection between me and him as a very thin and loosely-woven silver cord stretching between his mind and mine. "Got it!" I shrieked elatedly.

He smirked. "It's nothing to get THAT hyped up about! But ok, so you got it now, well done! Now, you can just simply clip the link with imaginary scissors or whatever imagery works best for you. You will feel the difference the second it's cut, as it sorta snaps back into you. Then, until we actively seek each other out with our links again, it won't automatically renew."

"Here goes nothing," I said, chewing on my bottom lip as I focused on making the connection go away. The thread felt so thin, that I could easily picture using a pair of nail clippers and just giving it a quick snip. It worked! My cord snapped back into my mind, and Matt's voice was no longer there.

I practiced the same technique with Jake's mindlink, and soon I was safely alone inside my head. *Well, if you don't count the multiple personalities. Har har.*

I paid attention to the way being alone felt compared to when someone else linked up with me. I wanted to immediately realize from now on if I was hooked to someone without my permission so I could sever it like Ruth had done earlier.

I noticed that when I mindlinked with someone there was a hollow feel to my mind. Like the connection was built in an echo chamber. And when I broke the link, my mind felt contained. I'd try to remember that feeling.

I couldn't wait to experiment with the others in the gang, but I didn't understand how I'd gotten automatically connected up with them in the first place.

"So, Matt," I said. "Can you explain to me how I joined up with you all in the first place if I'm supposed to have to forge the bond? I don't understand."

"Well, since our team is more or less a pack, we have a strong bond between us that we can access whenever we need or want to. Charlie, as team leader, can also override our bonds and communicate with us as one entity when time is of the essence. Since Charlie is the strongest neural networker amongst us, we think that when he sought out your mind and forged a link, he made us all latently linked to you too.

"But, until you reached your third chakra energy loop, none of us knew we were linked, and neither did you. If that's the case, you'll probably need to sever the flow with each of us, and after that it will become kinda' like a doorbell. The others 'knock' when they are wanting to link with us, and we can choose whether to extend and hook up or not. Does that make sense?"

Finally, someone who took the time to help me understand. "Yes, totally! I get it now. Thanks for clarifying. Maybe I'll have to upgrade you to luscious after all," I shamelessly flirted, giving him a big grin and a wink. *What's gotten into me, I'm supposed to be the shy one. Am I'm channeling Amaya or something?*

Speaking of Amaya, I was surprised she hadn't knocked down the door by now. I guess she'd be going to the movies with Tory and JC tonight. I was kinda sad about that; I hated giving up my BFF, normal teen angst time, but I knew we needed to keep moving forward here in order to get my dad off that chain.

That's my main priority, I reminded myself.

Now that Matt and Jake were outta my head, there was one bright spot—I could go back to lusting after them. *When did I become such a horndog?* Well, they were hubba hubba hawt, I'd give them that. Come to think of it, did Perrin have any unattractive people living in that dimension, because Charlie and every single member of the team were adorable. It was so unfair!

Not that I was entirely homely; I was not without my appeals, or so I'd been told. But I felt like an awkward and tongue-tied girl most of the time, while these peeps all seemed so sure of themselves, so together. Course, they'd probably been alive hundreds of years longer than me, so one would assume they'd get their act together a few times over in such a large stretch. *Yeah, there was that.*

I snuggled onto the couch between Matt and Jake, and we put on one of the Wolverine movies, the one where he goes feral. It seemed fitting. I was starting to feel safe with my team, and they with me, and although it was a very foreign feeling, it was not unwelcome.

I hoped Mom liked them too, because I didn't think they were going anywhere until we got this whole mess straightened out.

But do we have enough of Dad's money left to feed them all?

CHAPTER 15: DOWNTIME

W e'd only watched about ½ hour of the movie when the rest of the team returned, laughing and joking, and bearing umpteen bags of groceries. Yum! I couldn't wait to see what was for dinner. It was like having my own personal chef!

I popped off the couch to help put the food away, and decided to try my flash skills out again—although I really had no idea how I'd accomplished it the first time. I willed myself to the pantry and waited, but nothing happened; I ended up standing there looking like I was trying to fart or something. *Awkward.*

Luckily for me no one seemed to notice, so I grabbed Matt and pulled him off to the side. "Can you flash? And if so, how do you do it? I did it once this afternoon, but I just tried and nothing happened."

"Oh, I thought you were just constipated," Matt teased. I struggled to contain a smirk—because that was a good one—but I elbowed him in the ribs instead, and he held up his hands in surrender. "Ok, ok, I'll tell you. Remember the mindlink cord you saw earlier when we discussed how to stop the bond? You simply throw out the very same kind of thread—think of it more as a tool that we use to connect to anything—and let it pull you toward your intended destination. My mindpull is comparatively weak, but I can cover short distances without help. The stronger yours is the further you're capable of traveling. So, try again. Throw a line with your mind to the pantry, and let's see you flash over there, beautiful!"

I was so distracted that he'd called me beautiful that I almost lost my focus. *OMG. A super hot guy from another dimension just called me beautiful. Pinch me!*

I mentally slapped myself, threw out a cord, and disappeared into the pantry.

"Ha!" I shouted, throwing my arms up in a victory sign. "I did it all on my own! I stopped the mindlink with both Matt and Jake, and now I flashed without being in emotional anguish, too." As I spoke, I could feel the mental bond link up with the four remaining team members that I hadn't broken free of yet. I grabbed my mental nail clippers and snipped the links with Daniel, Curtis, Smith, and Bradley before they too got the privilege of partaking in my covetous crusade. There was only so much shame a girl could take in one day.

"Tada," I said, grinning and sweeping into a bow. Mom and Charlie had come out into the kitchen to check out the hullabaloo, so the whole team ending up clapping and cheering me on, Charlie beaming with pride and assuring me I'd put in a superb performance for my first day of training.

I knew I still had many mountains to climb, but at least I was heading in the direction my father needed for me to put an end to his misery.

We celebrated our advances of the past two days with a lavish dinner, Bradley and Tara outdoing themselves in the kitchen and putting the rest of us to work as their slaves. We made faux sour cream twice-baked potatoes, grilled asparagus spears, a savory gravy, homemade rolls, and the most amazing fake fried chicken to ever hit the planet. Seriously. It was kinda depressing that these folks had only been in their human form for one day, had never eaten vegan, and had put together a better meal than Mom and I had accomplished all year!

We didn't waste our time, or taste buds, whining about it, though. We dug in, gobbled it up, and fought for seconds.

There were even decadently-moist chocolate cupcakes with mint icing and chocolate ganache for dessert! *Ok, they're going to have to leave soon, or I'll be as big as a rhino. A pregnant rhino...with twins.*

Everyone ranted and raved and kissed the cooks, who blushed and eagerly started planning the next day's menu.

Mom, Charlie, the twins and I took more food and water to Wrath and filled him in on our day's progress. He was starting to come to himself in the blink of an eye whenever Charlie and I got within range, and I was grateful. I hated feeling afraid of my own father; even though I knew it wasn't his fault, the tremors still came.

I chose not to snip the bonds with Randulf because I was worried about being able to relink with him in his feral state. I figured it would be smarter to just be in place when he came to and not have to count on my newby skills in time of crisis.

Charlie and I were realizing we had a unique bond, but we hadn't exactly figured out the what or why yet. I was able to snip my connection to him, but like with his pack, he could override it in time of need and appear in my mind. I was ok with that, since I wholly trusted him, and he was my favorite gay uncle.

"I'm not gay, for the 100th time," came his voice in my mind, a tad indignantly. "Not that there's anything wrong with that," he winked and smiled in spite of himself, and I grinned back. I was impressed he even knew or understood the catchphrase from the Seinfeld TV series, given that he'd been in cat form most of his time on earth in this century. But, then again, Charlie was a surprising man.

"We need to link up with your father together, so don't get angry that I'm in your head, Young One," he said. "King, are you there?"

"Yes, Charles, I'm here." He'd just finished scarfing down the food we'd brought. Mom looked at him so despairingly that I could tell she wanted to grab him and run off, somehow finding a way to make this better, to escape. I had to look away from the raw emotion splashed across her face. They were both a bit pitiful at this point, and I wasn't used to feeling that kind of emotion toward my parents. I wanted THEM to be the strong ones—but now it seemed like it was up to me.

We discussed the progress we'd made today, and the suggestion that had come up over dinner. "Your Highness, we'd like to try an experiment," Charlie explained. "You say this chain is somehow magically connected to you and you are unable to break it, is that correct?"

"As far as I can tell, yes."

"Our theory is that the chain is a physical manifestation of our mindlinks. That it is somehow linking both to you and an unknown object or force that your kidnappers have devised. Are you following me so far?"

Both Wrath and I nodded.

"So we'd like Baylee and I to combine our strengths

together in an attempt to break it, given that in our presence you're able to block at least some of the chain's dominance over you. Do you want to try it now? Are you ready?"

"As I'll ever be. Please proceed."

Charlie and I both grabbed a piece of the chain—Charlie closest to Wrath and I nearer the ground anchor—and tugged with all our might.

Nothing happened. *Bummer. So much for super-strength.*

We tried again and again, but there never seemed to be a weakening in the structure of the chain. We finally gave up for the night when Randulf informed us he thought it was getting close to the time his captors came to the house.

I was disheartened. I had failed at my first big assignment, already. That hadn't taken long.

Matt and Jake stayed behind, hiding themselves in the shadows of the house and well away from Wrath's reach or smell, but close enough to get eyes on whoever might show up tonight.

I hated leaving all three of them in what felt like a powder keg situation, but I knew we all had our parts to play, and each was willing and eager to do their share.

Mom gave Dad a huge kiss right on the snout, and he rubbed his muzzle along her arm, instructing me to tell her that he loved her. Her eyes misted up, and giving him a final "I love you, too," she turned and sprinted back toward the house.

Charlie and I had to flash to keep up with her.

Chapter 16: Kidnapped

I awoke to the sounds of raised voices from downstairs, and my heart about burst through my chest cavity and fell out onto the floor. I jumped out of bed and flashed myself downstairs without even being fully cognizant of what I was doing. *Pretty cool.*

I should have been smarter, though, I belatedly realized, since I had no idea what I was flashing myself into. *Not so cool after all.*

I was lucky—this time—that I didn't arrive into the middle of something I couldn't handle. There appeared to be only "my" people in the room, yet everyone was panicking and talking over each other. I had no idea what was going on.

Mom wasn't around.

"Um, guys," I yelled. No one stopped talking or listened to me. I ripped out my best whistle. Still nothing. Then it dawned on me that maybe I could reach into their heads with mindlink the way Charlie could. I mean, if I was supposed to be the big bad warrior who went up against the scion, then shouldn't I be able to connect with all my teammates simultaneously too?

With no time to lose, I thrust my threads out toward every member of the clan. I had no idea what it would feel like if I were successful, but I gave a mindyell just in case. "Warriors! Stand down! Would someone please share with me why we're panicking!"

Instantly the room quieted and every eye turned toward me. Even the dogs. *Huh. Could I reach into their minds too? Now that would be wicked!*

Charlie responded. "Well, it seems you're definitely the one we've been seeking if you can plunge into all our heads without our permission. Let's discuss the proper etiquette when taking such actions, such as NOT raising your voice. Ouch." He rubbed his ear, like I'd screamed directly into it.

I felt shame for a second, like I'd done something wrong, but then I decided BS to that. "Look, if you're all down here shrieking at 2:00 a.m., then that constitutes an emergency situation in my book, and you can all just deal with me plunging into your heads. Now, please enlighten me as to the panicked state, so I can either join in or help figure out how to fix it."

They all looked at my like I had five heads or something. *What? I'm coming into my own, that's all, people. Get a grip. Oops, did they hear that?* I needed a better handle of this particular skill.

Jake was the first to speak, and I saw him mentally trying to hold himself together. "Matt's disappeared; I think he was kidnapped. We were watching the house from the shadows, and attempting to make sure Wrath didn't catch wind of us. After you left he went feral again. He kept growling as he sniffed the air, trying to figure out where we were hiding. It was really freaky, like he was tracking us even though he couldn't see us."

He paused, and Curtis put a comforting hand on his

shoulder. "Then we heard something from the front of the house, so Matt went to investigate. There was a scuffle, and then a scream I'm sure was his, and then silence. I ran around to engage the enemy, but found no one. Matt had disappeared, and the vicinity was barren. Wrath was going crazy out back on his chain, making it hard to listen for any other noises. I was hesitant to break into the house without backup, so I ran back here to get help. That's where we're at now."

Daniel, the de facto military leader of the clan, spoke up. "They are either luring us into a trap, or they don't know we're here yet and think they've just caught one intruder. Trouble is, if these ninjas, or whoever they are, are from Perrin, they'll know that Matt is too. Which makes it a whole new ballgame."

"Well, what do we do, then? We can't leave him there. What's our plan for getting him out? And where's Mom?"

Charlie piped up. "I put a deep sleep suggestion, called a mindbind, into your mother as soon as Jake rushed in, so she's perfectly fine but slumbering peacefully upstairs. We'll all go with the exception of Smith and Tara, who will stay here to guard Candice and the property. You and I will come from the back to bring Wrath out of his feral state and see if he knows anything. Rebecca and Ruth will stand guard with us, while Daniel, Curtis, Bradley, and Jake break in through the front. We have yet to be able to arm ourselves with anything but the weapons our gifts bring us, so don't hesitate to use them as needed; we have no idea what we're up against.

"Let us go, mates. Link up with the team, and keep everyone apprised of your status every step of the way. Best of luck, everyone."

I flashed back upstairs and threw on some black attire. *If I'm gonna be covert, I gotta look the part. For once Mom couldn't bitch that I was wearing all black.* I was grateful she wasn't awake, or I'd have to deal with freaked out worry-mom too. *No thanks on that. I've got enough on my plate.*

The others had dressed quickly and were waiting for me by the door. Daniel came through the mindlink. "From this point on, radio silence. Questions?" We shook our heads. "Then, flash!"

The four of us appeared deep in the shadows of the alley, about ten yards behind Wrath. He lay quietly as if asleep, but immediately heard us and his ears pricked up, turning in our direction.

We hadn't even moved from our spot yet before his voice was in my head. "Stay where you are. I sense danger, and I'm not sure which direction it's coming from. Allow me to work my magic a minute so I can get a handle on it. On the bright side, my recall from feral is becoming much quicker now. The second I feel you and Charlie here together, it pops me back into myself."

We nodded but otherwise stayed silent, terrified to move a muscle. Wrath slowly rose and stretched, as if he were just any normal dog waking from a nap. We assumed whoever had kidnapped and tethered him to them was not in his head, and had no idea that he was now coming back to himself at times. That assumption seemed a bit sketchy to me.

He walked stiffly around the circumference where the years had worn the path mapped by his paws. I had to look away. It was so awful to contemplate that life, an existence confined to a tiny space, each moment enduring the indignity of dragging a logging chain in his wake.

Humanity was disgusting in its inhumanity.

Weather would never be his friend living out here. The number of perfect days per year probably numbered less than thirty, leaving 330 days with potential for basic survival challenges. Extremes could fluctuate depending on the season here in Northern Virginia, but he'd often have to deal with heat, cold, wind, rain, or snow, on top of the general misery of living as a chained, feral dog.

We were only a week away from Christmas break, and temps in the state had been mild this winter, but we were still looking at an overnight drop to 35 degrees. Wrath had a rickety, broken down shelter—if one could even call it that—and I'd never seen him bother going inside it. That's the reality of the life to which my father had been sentenced.

Charlie prompted him. "Anything yet?" I pulled myself from my inner rant.

"Nope. I can sense that someone has been here, though. I can hear your men at the front of the house, too. What's happened?"

"Do you remember anything from tonight, Dad?" I asked. "Matt has disappeared. He and Jake were staking out the house when they heard a noise. When Matt went to investigate something happened to him, and he seems to have been nabbed. They're breaking into the building now to search for him."

Wrath shook his head sadly. "I'm sorry, I feel so useless in my feral state. It's like I have a barrier in my brain when I turn, and even though I must be observant of my surroundings, when I come back to myself I can't access those memories. Charlie, I wonder if you'd be able to dig around in there and see if you can find anything? We both have mindgrind abilities; maybe you can get past the blockage to see more."

"I'll try, your Highness. Going in now, Sir." Charlie leaned against the wall of the shed we were hiding behind. He got a look of intense concentration on his face, and I linked up with him so I could see what he was seeing. He was flipping quickly through Randulf's memories, and I got glimpses of some of him with my mom when he was in human form. I wanted to stop and watch them, but we had more important things to do, and maybe it was intrusive anyway.

He arrived at the moment Randulf turned feral, and the memories changed to just random pictures that didn't flow together or make any sense. Suddenly we hit a wall, and we couldn't see anything further after that. Dammit!

"Interesting, Sire," said Charlie. "We can see when you first turned feral, but then we too were blocked from going any further. I believe that whoever kidnapped you put that barricade in your brain, so the problem is not from the feral state, per se. We were able to see images from your time as a feral before you were taken, but not since. I believe we are dealing with a much more sophisticated kidnapping system than I had previously given them credit for. I'm going to go over everything we know tonight with Tara, as she has a very lovely scientific mind. She may be able to help us see something we're missing."

Just then Curtis came on the mindline (*I crack myself up sometimes*) from the front of the house. "Rebecca, Ruth, come quick! We found him, but there's something off about his aura, and he's passed out."

The twins took off around the side of the house, and although I longed to follow after them, I knew I couldn't leave Wrath or he'd revert to feral again. I realized I could link up with them and at least be privy to what was going on that way, so I threw out a line to each. They didn't protest; maybe they were getting used to the idea of me in their heads, or trusted me a little more now that they were getting to know me.

I didn't want to be intrusive, but I wondered what else I could do once I was in there. After seeing Charlie go through Randulf's head, I was curious what I was capable of. "Ruth, Rebecca, is it ok if I try to access the visuals you're seeing too? I believe if they're being logged in your mind, I can in effect watch what's happening through your eyes."

Ruth made noises like she wasn't too thrilled about the idea, but Rebecca didn't mind, stating that Charlie often did the same thing when they were on mission. I was beginning to feel like Ruth had something against me—but maybe she was just a very private person.

I'm obviously trying to reassure myself that I'm not hated—I should probably just get used to it instead. I doubted that my position would make me Ms. Popular.

Rebecca reminded Ruth through the link that the team understood and supported the need for their command to see as much as possible in any given situation, and this included mindlink when necessary. Since I would be in a leadership position in the very near future, Rebecca considered this my training period, and invited and accepted me into her link to watch the visuals as they occurred. Ruth still held back.

As the two women rounded the corner, they saw Jake and Curtis carrying Matt upright between them, quickly moving him to the side of the house and out of the glare of the streetlight. He still looked out of it, and the men were worried that he wasn't coming to.

Even though it was easier for Ruth to read auras without synthetic fabrics in her way, we couldn't strip Matt down in the middle of town, so she did her best to read him through his clothing. Rebecca was talented with auras, too; she could see them as well as Ruth could, but Ruth had an edge on interpreting and hand-working within the energy of the aura.

Through Rebecca's eyes I noticed that Matt's aura was a muddy brown, and this color was at its most concentrated on the left side of his neck. She explained that he normally had a fairly consistent yellow aura, very close to the color of mine we'd seen today. Something was definitely wrong.

"Can you flash him back to the house?" Ruth asked. The guys all shook their heads. Most of the team could easily carry themselves that far or further, but they got into trouble when they had to carry their wounded. Charlie was the best with that, followed by Smith, who was guarding mom and the house. *Shoot, Smith should have been here. Poor planning on our parts.*

Charlie chimed in. "Just stay in the shadows for a moment, team, we'll be there in a second. Your Highness, we have Matt, but he's injured, and we need to get him back to Baylee's house. We'll come back in the morning with more food and to update you on what we've learned between now and then."

"Thank you, Charlie," Randulf said bitterly. "I hate being trapped here and unable to help, but I trust you and Baylee will soon find a path to free me; then we can go after these bastards for what they've done and propose to do to our world. Until tomorrow."

I awkwardly patted Wrath on the head and pulled my best determined face. "We WILL free you, Father. You have our word."

We immediately flashed to the side of our teammates, and Charlie hauled all six of us home with him as one. Impressive! I hoped I could be that good one day.

I unlinked from the group, relieved to be free of the mental entanglements, and popped myself upstairs for a quick shower. I felt so grimy, but they kept wearing me out and then I ended up falling into bed without getting clean first. *Yuk.*

I didn't want to miss anything, though, so I hurriedly washed off the top layer of dirt and raced back downstairs. *At least I feel human again, and less like the roadkill I was always lamenting.*

Matt was laid out on the couch, and Ruth and Tara were examining him. It seemed that Ruth was more of a psychic surgeon, taking care of anything on the energy level, and Tara was the physical surgeon. In this case both of their skillsets were needed, and they deliberated over the cause of the brown muddy aura in his neck area.

I walked over to take a look for myself, and immediately saw what they were going on about. His aura had turned into a sickly, baby diarrhea yellow-brown everywhere but the left side of his neck. There it was the color of mud, and was swirling about in a dizzying fashion.

There was also a rather nasty protrusion in that spot, which Ruth felt needed to come out ASAP. Tara was erring on the side of caution, however, and argued that if whatever was in there were dangerous, removing it without understanding what we were dealing with could cause him further harm. And maybe us, too.

My gut urged me to tell them to get it out, so I decided to

speak up. *I hope I'm not wrong, for criminy's sake. That's all I need, more guilt.*

"Hey, guys, I don't know if this is part of my skillset or what, but my third chakra is letting me know quite clearly that that thing needs to be removed. NOW. Take it for what it's worth. But that's the message I'm getting loud and clear."

"Then we've reached a consensus," Charlie exclaimed. "I too believe it needs to be extricated immediately. Tara, shall I procure you a knife from the kitchen?"

I almost threw up in my mouth a little. "Um, seriously, guys, we can't do any better than a kitchen knife? You don't have, like, a doctor's kit or something?"

Tara looked at me coolly. "Now where would I have put that in my kitty suit, dear? I would love to purchase one tomorrow as we have an obvious need, but for tonight we must make do with what we have."

I rushed over to the kitchen and dug out both the peroxide and the rubbing alcohol. I really didn't know which one was best, so I poured them both in turn over our sharpest knife, and carried the knife, the peroxide, the alcohol, and a couple towels back into the room with me. I also sanitized Matt's skin before I'd let Tara anywhere near him, which she found amusing. She reminded me that they are immortals, and as such heal quite quickly from any kind of incision or injury. It was very rare for them to suffer an infection as a result of a wound.

Oh, shiza. I forgot about that.

I tried not to look as she sliced Matt's neck open, but curiosity got the better of me. The second she made the cuts around the protruding object, a chip fell out onto the towel. Not a potato chip, obviously, but some kind of microchip or tracking device. I wasn't an expert on these kinds of things, but I imagined Curtis would be all over it.

I was told he was the resident tech guy.

Curtis grabbed it up eagerly and examined it closely, putting in a request with management (aka, me) for a magnifying glass. That was old school, though, and we didn't even have one in the house; I pulled out my iPhone and we used the magnifying app instead.

He was suitably impressed with my human technology and vowed to study it further at his first opportunity, but for now made do with quietly analyzing the implant for a good two minutes before he finally looked up. "It's obviously a chip, but more like a transmitter than a computer chip. I'm worried it was set up to collect his thoughts, or the information and data he gathers from wherever he is, and send it to the enemy. I'm also afraid that means they're onto us, and were using him as an unwitting mole to infiltrate our group and find out what we know and what actions we're contemplating."

We looked at each other, wide-eyed and scared.

It was at that moment that Matt opened his eyes and moaned.

CHAPTER 17: UP A CREEK

I would vehemently deny that I got a little verklempt when I saw Matt awake; there was just a dog hair in my eye, that's all. *Yeah, that's it.* It's not like I had a tiny crush on him or anything, *eh-hem*, but the thought of any member of our team going down would be a painful one.

And especially one as yummy as him, with those dark good looks, deep chocolate eyes, and shoulder-length shiny curls. That boy was man-candy to the max, I'm not gonna lie.

I felt like Matt and I were starting to bond, too, and if that led to a little shameless flirting on occasion, I'd be the last one in that complaint line.

Matt looked directly at me and asked, "Is everyone ok? I think I had some bad dreams. Why is everyone looking at me?"

Tara took the lead, deep into her doctor role. "Matt, what's the last thing you remember?"

"Hmm," he said, squishing up his eyes and trying to think back. "Jake and I were standing in the shadows of the house when we heard a sound up front. I snuck around the corner instead of flashing so that I didn't end up in the middle of something dangerous. I wanted to get a look first."

He stopped, wrinkling his forehead in thought. "Um . . . it's like there's a blank spot that I can't access now." Charlie and I looked at each other.

"The same thing keeps happening to Wrath, too," I mindlinked to him. He simply nodded his head, worried.

"I remember seeing black shadowy figures coming toward me, and fast. I was trying to ascertain if they were human or something 'other,' when I was grabbed hard and yanked into the front yard. I took a swing, saw a blinding light, and that was it for me. Next thing I remember I'm waking up right now with you all staring at me like I have cooties crawling out of my hair or something. Seriously, it's weird, people. Back off! Nothing more to see here!"

We all backed up a few paces, giving Mr. Grumpypants a little room to breathe. It was weird not knowing what to make of this latest information, or lack thereof. It felt like our enemy was toying with us, and we were left operating in the dark. No one wanted to tell Matt that he'd been invasively cut open and had a chip implanted in his neck. He needed a little time to regroup for that one.

Tara continued. "Well, how are you feeling physically right now? Do you think you can sit up, eat?"

Matt looked at me, holding his hand out with a piteous expression on his face. "If Miss Baylee would deign to escort me, I will attempt to make my way to the kitchen and outeat even our resident foodie, Bradley Lardbutt."

"Ha, in your dreams, little boy," Bradley retorted, beelining it for the kitchen.

I playfully grabbed Matt's hand and gave him a good jerk, pulling him all the way off the couch and into the air. *Oops, embarrassing! Add my newfound strength to the list of things*

I need to get a handle on.

I quickly set him down and endeavored to better play along, taking his arm gallantly in mine. "Allow me, Mr. Matthew. And what dost thy tastebuds require in the way of nourishment this evening, kind sir?"

Bradley took his food very seriously. "Since it's like 5:00 a.m. now, maybe we should do the big breakfast thing and discuss our options before Candice wakes up. Her mindbind will probably last only another hour or so. Who wants to help cook?"

Tara jumped in, of course, and the two of them set off on a cooking frenzy that dragged the rest of us along for the ride. We might not have been the best of chefs, but we all loved to eat, and so became their willing servants with eyes firmly set on the food prize at the end of our work shift. The two of them had pored over Mom's cookbooks when they weren't working the mission and highlighted a bunch of recipes they wanted to make.

We settled on homemade crepes with spinach and Vegg scramble and hollandaise sauce, and then followed that up with dessert crepes with Tofutti cream cheese and crushed and sweetened raspberry topping.

YUM! I have got to find a way to kidnap these two and make them cook for me for the rest of my life, I mused. *And maybe Matt too, as I am in need of eye-candy and a flirtation device.*

Matt was the first to declare himself too full to stuff in even one more smidge. It was then that Charlie broke the news to him about his implant.

He was livid, as expected—as any of us would have been. To be violated in that manner, to not even understand what had been done to him or why, was a difficult pill to swallow.

This engendered a lively discussion about who could be behind this, and how we were going to go about finding out more. It seemed that both Wrath and Matt had memory blocks that prohibited us from seeing behind the embedded barricade.

And they were the only two who'd seen these people. *Yeah, frustrating.*

Daniel had been pretty quiet throughout the discussion. I was learning that, as the military commander type, he had a habit of listening first, processing everything he'd heard, and only then coming up with his own strategic input. He liked to get all his facts lined up and wait for the plan that made the most sense to come to him. I respected him for that.

"Since we didn't get time to explore that house tonight, I think we have no other choice but to break in again tomorrow and go over it inch by inch. There's got to be some clue in there as to the identity of the evil mastermind. Why else would Wrath be chained at that particular house?"

He scratched his chin. "He can't remember much, but he does believe he's guarding something. We've got to look for this something—whatever it is—and remove it, maybe flash it back to Perrin. It's obviously of some import to those seeking to do harm to our realm. That alone makes its retrieval a number one priority."

We all nodded our agreement.

Charlie stood, stretching tiredly. "Well, let's all grab a couple hours of much-needed rest, and convene back here at 10:00 a.m. I'll let Candice know what happened last night, and why we are all sleeping now—and that we saved her some breakfast, so she won't be too mad at us!"

I interrupted. "Mom normally goes out to breakfast with her friend Janie on Sundays, then they do a movie and afterward go for a run or hit the gym. It's their ritual. Charlie, if you can talk her into spending some quality time with her bestie while we figure out how to rescue Wrath, at least she won't be here worrying about us all day. Maybe do a little mindgrind persuasion if necessary?" *Desperate times and all.* He nodded.

"I'm hitting the sack," I yawned. "If you need me, you know where to find me."

I trudged wearily up the stairs. *This lack of sleep is really starting to mess with me. As well as the lack of information,* I lamented. *I feel like we're running blindly into a maze with a king cobra waiting to strike at every turn. Not a pleasant feeling.*

I spent longer than usual in the shower, the warm water running over my head and body encasing me in an imagined cocoon of safety.

Ah, I needed this. Truth be told, I hadn't felt safe since I met my new family on Friday morning. I had a feeling safety was a thing of the past.

My mind ran over all that had happened in the last two days, and I couldn't shake the feeling that there was a giant clue I was missing. But what was it?

Why was my father chained only two blocks from me? Does the enemy know that I exist and where I am, or is this all just some massive coincidence?

Why does Wrath only become Randulf in the presence of both Charlie and myself? Why can't we break his chain, when we both have super-strength?

My gut started churning, like it wanted me to PAY

ATTENTION and NOW. *Ok*, I told it. *I'm all ears. Whatcha got for me?* After my instinct had proven correct with Matt earlier, I decided my newly-opened third chakra was smarter than me, and I should just shut up and fall in line. I brought my attention to my solar plexus, waiting expectantly for enlightenment.

It did not disappoint. There were quick flashes of intuition, visual images reminding me of the process of learning to mindlink with everyone, focusing in on the connection points of the tethers between our minds. *Yeah, got it, tethers.* The next image illustrated my mental clipping of the tethers to unlink them. *Ok, I snip the cords. Yep.*

The third image compared the thin links going between our minds for communication with the thick chain running from the ground post up to Wrath's neck. *So, Wrath's chain is more or less a physical manifestation of the linking tethers. I think we'd already gotten that much, but go on . . .*

And then the last image materialized, and I was blown away by the simplicity of the answer that we'd somehow missed. *Duh! Of course!* Pulling on the tethers in our minds does nothing to them. They only act like rubber bands and bounce right back into position.

So us PULLING on Wrath's chain did nothing but encourage it to stubbornly hold to its bond with him.

The chain had to be clipped!

It has to be clipped! I didn't yet know how to do that, whether it was a physical or mental clipping that had to occur to break that chain, but I knew I was onto something. Well, my gut was anyway. *Woohoo!*

I jumped out of the shower and quickly toweled off, slipping into my sweats and sleep-T. I wanted to go look for

Charlie, but realized he was probably already asleep himself. I knew he hadn't been getting much rest either.

I'd wait until we met at 10:00 a.m. to give him the good news, and let him take it from there. I slid gratefully under my covers, calling BooBoo to come cuddle his momma. I feel asleep with him in my arms and a smile on my face.

CHAPTER 18: CLIPPING PATH

Mom had already left to meet Janie at their favorite breakfast spot, Hidden Jules Café, when we all once again amassed in the kitchen. I breathed a sigh of relief. At least I didn't have to deal with her fussing and worrying over me today. I knew I was in good hands with Charlie and his team, and if anything happened, we would all get through it together.

With Mom being all human (*Ok, that's just a weird thing to say*) she really couldn't assist us anyway, and would have slowed us down since we planned to flash as much as possible to get in and out without anyone seeing us.

I had texts from both her and Amaya. Mom's were all lovey-dovey and smarmy, telling me to stay safe and she'd see me later—my typical loving "Make Wise Choices" Mom. Amaya was getting more pissed by the day at my continued absence, and I knew I was going to be in for it tomorrow morning at school.

God help me. The Wrath of Dog has nothing on The Wrath of Amaya.

The company excuse was wearing thin, but I needed to hold her off for just one more day. This world I'd somehow ended up in was too dangerous for her, and I couldn't bear it if something happened to her.

The biggest part of me wished she was here with me right now, going through all this by my side. I was both funner and funnier with her around (*at least I thought so*), and our snarky comments played off one another, often ending with us holding our stomachs from all the laughing. She made me see the humor in the toughest of times, an invaluable trait in a best friend.

I missed her.

I didn't know if I'd ever be able to bring her into my world, and it was a sobering thought. A future without my best friend was not a future I wanted to face.

I pulled myself away from my glum musings and addressed Charlie about my idea for the chain. "Charlie, my third chakra is showing me we need to clip the chain, not pull it; that it's a physical manifestation of the tethers we use to communicate and flash ourselves between places. The only thing I don't understand is if we have to physically snip it, somehow, or if it's a mental thing. Thoughts?"

"Hmmm," he replied. "Nicely done, Baylee." He rubbed his chin, looking around at the others. "Team, we haven't encountered anything like this before; what do you think? Mental clipping or physical clipping, for the chain? And if physical, what could we possibly use that would get through something that thick?"

Now it was Smith's turn to take center stage, as he was their go-to mechanical guy. The brawn of the bunch, Smith was super smart but not in the book or computer way; he was the tools and "all things handiworky" type. He was the only other team member, besides Charlie, who could carry someone else with him when he flashed. This was totally his arena.

He ran his fingers through his blonde locks, the brown around his ears and the cornflower blue of his eyes drawing my attention. *I love how their colors in human form are so reflective of their cat forms. It's fascinating. I wonder if I can turn into anything? Wouldn't that be the shit?*

I know, I know. Mom wants me to lay off the swearing, but with my new lifestyle, I think swearing is going to be par for the course. She'd just better get used to it.

"My guess is that we're going to need a combination of the mental and the physical planes to get through that thick steel. I don't think either can cut it by itself, so let's try both together. I saw a pair of gardening shears in the garage. Let me grab those, and we'll hit the back alley first to try to free Wrath before going inside."

We all murmured our agreement, while he flashed to the garage. He was back momentarily with both a pruning saw and the shears he'd mentioned, handing me the shears and Charlie the saw.

"I really don't think you'll need both," Smith continued, shouldering a backpack he'd found in the garage to carry any evidence we came across. "But let's take them in case. I know that Baylee said she uses clippers when she cuts the tethers in her mind, while Charlie uses a mental knife. Best to have both on hand."

We readied ourselves, donning thicker jackets and shoes, as the Virginia Decembers tended to be quite frigid. This time Rebecca and Ruth stayed behind to guard the homestead and make sure we had no nasty surprises to come home to. We didn't know how much Wrath's captors knew about us, which put us at a disadvantage; we couldn't trust leaving our base unwatched.

Daniel flashed to the alleyway near Wrath and back quickly to make sure we were clear. This team was so in sync with each other and so in tune with their abilities that I never grew tired of watching them; I was developing a furtive desire to be part of their pack. Daniel made sure everyone was ready, gave a nod, and as one we flashed to just beyond Wrath's reach, materializing in the shadow of the nearby shed.

Wrath leapt up, growling, but by the time his paws touched the ground again he had come into his Randulf-mind.

"Hello, my beautiful daughter," he said, warmly. "I'm so glad you came back. Did you bring food and water?"

I looked guiltily around at the others, because in truth I'd been so excited about the possibility of freeing Wrath that I'd completely forgotten to pack up the essentials. By the time I'd begun to sheepishly confess my forgetfulness, Tara had flashed to the house and back with both the morning's leftover breakfast and a gallon of water.

She shyly offered them to Wrath, and he indicated his bowls with his snout. She hurried over and filled both bowls to the brim, Wrath immediately and unceremoniously falling to ravenously inhaling the food and water.

The team seemed uncomfortable seeing their King in such a state, but Randulf wasn't bothered by their discomfort. He'd been living as a wild, chained animal for so long that his memories of being clean and, well, Kingly, seemed distant and faded by now.

After he'd finished up, I relayed our good news. He glanced at me skeptically out of the corner of one eye, dryly remarking to Charlie. "How do you feel about it, Charles? Do you think it will work?"

"I'm optimistic, sire. Our first goal while here is to break the chain away from its base anchor. Then when we are safely back home we will endeavor to remove it entirely from your neck. Does that sound reasonable?"

"Well, let's get on with it, then," the King grumbled, like he was afraid to hope. "If you can free me, we need to immediately flash inside and take a look around. Maybe I can get a sense of what I'm here to guard and how dangerous it is. I don't believe there's anyone inside now, but I can't make any promises."

Charlie and I assumed the same ready stance we had last evening. This time we both held the chain in one hand, and gripped the shears in the other. It was awkward, but doable. Charlie instructed, "I want us to try to clip it mentally first. If that doesn't work, then we put the shears to use on the physical plane. Got it?"

I nodded my head, already concentrating. My gut told me we were on the right track, but there was something still gnawing at me. We pictured the chain as a tether, and while I clipped it, Charlie sliced through it mentally with a knife. After a minute of mental anguish I felt the chain heating my hand—so we'd made progress—but we were going to have to bring the shears to bear too. We pulled both ends of the chain taut, and pictured snipping through the chain while simultaneously applying pressure with the shears.

The area around the pruners turned red hot and the steel melted, dripping into a pool on the ground. Within seconds the links had all but disintegrated—and Wrath was finally FREE! After 18 years!

I still held the side of the chain that was tethered to my father, making do with it as a leash until we got home.

Charlie was holding the end of the chain that burrowed into the ground anchor, and hastily dropped it with a look of horror on his face.

I raised my arms over my head to celebrate just as Charlie reached his arm out toward me; it was in that moment that I felt my mind go feral.

Aw, this is the part that was nagging at me, I realized as my sense of self fell away. *What would happen to the three of us after we cut the chain if this tether was in fact a massive conduit?*

Chapter 19: Pandemonium

On some level I understood what was happening, but was helpless to stop it. Because the chain was now an amplified version of the threads that normally linked our minds, I was immediately sucked into Wrath's feral state. Without Charlie involved in our triad, not only did Wrath go back to feral, but he dragged me along with him.

Randulf had been immortal for a long, long time (I didn't yet know exactly how long that had been) and had become King because he bore the fiercest mental powers in the dimension. As his daughter, and an already-strong and growing stronger half-Perrinite myself, I was still no match for him, and was unprepared for the sheer force of will that slammed into me.

I became a raging lunatic, at least inside my head, and had no idea what was happening on the outside. I could see, but nothing made sense; there were visual images of people and objects, but they held no names, bore no meanings. I could sense danger all around me, and I wanted nothing more than to slash and rip and claw, maim and destroy, eliminate every threat to my safety, my life.

I was linked to Wrath, and he to me, and we were of one mind. I was no longer aware I was holding onto a chain, that

I was a human, that he was a dog. There was only bloodlust and hate, mayhem and malevolence.

I hung on, with Wrath yanking me toward Daniel and Curtis, murder and hostility the only two things on his mind. Sounded good to me. Their eyes went wide, and they tried to flash out of the way, but Wrath was too fast, grabbing Daniel by the leg with his massive jaws. I lashed out at Curtis, and he darted behind me, trying to pull me away from the chain.

It didn't work. I had become physically attached to it.

Daniel screamed, and the sound of his pain only upped the bloodlust careening through my brain. The rest of the team had descended on the King, trying to force him to release Daniel, while Charlie ran to me and attempted to disengage me from the links.

When Charlie touched me I briefly came back to myself, enough to get an inkling of what was happening and get a sense of our general descent into madness. I tried to drop the chain, but my hands were affixed, and no amount of tugging could remove them.

Wrath was still shaking Daniel, and the team was still shaking Wrath.

Mayhem reigned.

Then Charlie took a risk, the only move open to him that had a hope of ending this insanity. He took hold of the chain beside me, knowing full well he too could end up pulled into the same barbaric matrix that encircled Wrath and me.

It was our only chance.

At first it was shaky. I could feel my mind going in and out of feral, and it seemed the chain was magnifying the King's already-strong powers. My gut felt the dark tentacles as they reached out and tried to yank me back in.

But I resisted, well aware that this was life and death for me, and maybe even Charlie and his team if the trauma was too deep and fast for their systems to rebuild. We had no choice but to overcome. Together, Charlie and I were able to shore up and augment our normal mental tether, pour that combined energy into the chain links, and repulse the feral that was still fighting to overpower us.

Finally, it worked. Wrath sank to the ground, limp, and released Daniel's leg from his massive jaws. Daniel rolled over in agony, clutching his knee, while blood seeped from multiple wounds, soaking his pants and the soil beneath. Smith gingerly picked him up and he and Tara flashed back to the house to begin immediate trauma care.

Smith was back in an instant and ready for anything, landing in fight stance; but by then the King and I had ourselves well enough in hand, and everyone was starting to calm down and breathe again.

Charlie and I still shared the chain between us, not knowing if we remained physically attached; or, if we could release it, what would happen to the King. We stood together as an awkward threesome.

"Well, I am sorry, Your Highness, I should have realized the implications of the chain working as a conductor, but it never entered my mind. I find myself in unexplored territory here, and I am afraid this will not be the last mistake we make throughout this process. How are you?" Charlie asked.

Randulf sighed. "I'm doing fine, just disappointed in myself for hurting Daniel. When I go to the feral side, all I want to do is annihilate whatever unfortunate being is exposed within my field of vision. I'm nothing more than a monster without empathy or understanding," he said, disgust and sorrow etched in his voice.

"I can vouch for that," I said, shuddering. "I was in there with you, and I wanted to do all the same things. Murder and mayhem. I don't know how you've lived with this for so long. I'm sorry, Father. Something was nagging at me about our plan, but I couldn't put my finger on it. It was only after we sliced the tether that I realized we hadn't taken the time to think about what would come after. Suffice it to say, this was a valuable lesson for all of us."

He rubbed his face against my black pants in the only way he was currently able to show affection. I tried not to flinch back, not to be afraid of my own father. *I'm gonna need a shrink, ASAP. And hopefully not one like that crazy psycho on Suicide Squad.* "It's not your fault, Baylee. You had no way of knowing. You're young, and you've only been exposed to our world for two days. The onus is on us to do better in the future."

It was decided that both Charlie and I should keep our hands on the chain until we got back to the house and figured out what came next. Our hold on Wrath's sanity seemed all too tenuous to test the waters without a safe location in which to do so.

In the meantime, we needed to regroup and get into that building Wrath was guarding ASAP. What was in there?

We took stock of our situation, with Charlie taking over as lead since Daniel was down for the count. "So, has anyone been watching the house and ensuring we weren't seen or heard during this ghastly debacle?"

Bradley piped up. "I threw up a mindchime around us as soon as things went haywire, Charlie," said my favorite brown tabby-looking foodie.

"I'm sorry, you said mindchime? What in all that is consecrated is that supposed to mean?" *I can see I'm gonna need a list of all possible abilities and which clan mate has which skills.*

"Oh, right, you're not familiar with our catalogue of funky names for things. Mindchime is the act of creating a sound perimeter, so that noises don't get in or out of the set area. Kinda like a sound bubble, I'd guess. That way the neighbors can't hear us when things get hairy—which turned out to be for the best given Daniel's shrieking. The cops would surely be here by now otherwise."

"Yeah, you're right about that," I said, relieved to know the neighbors hadn't been alerted. "Thank you for saving our hides. Charlie, how do we move on from here? Wrath, do you sense anyone inside the house? Is it safe for us to go in?" I was proud of myself for not falling to pieces.

Not right now, later. I reasoned that by attempting some semblance of leadership, I could learn both how to take charge when needed and take my focus off thoughts of the lunacy I'd just experienced.

Wrath stilled, concentrating. He lifted his head and sniffed the breeze, a frown wrinkling his doggie brow. "I'm not sensing anything, but we need to be on high alert. I'd expect them to have cameras or alarms or something inside as well."

Charlie signaled for us to move out, and we slunk single file around the side of the house. He alerted me that he'd been actively throwing out suggestions to look the other way to any passersby since it was still daylight, and assured me we should be able to reach the side door unnoticed.

Once there, Wrath came back online. "Since I can't even remember the last time I was out of that backyard, my senses are being overwhelmed with new sights and smells. But my instinct is telling me that we need to go in through the front door. Does anyone else have a feeling about this?"

My gut was screaming the same. "Yep, me too," I included everyone in my reply, throwing out tethers. "Something isn't right about this side door, peeps. I know it would be easier, but we need to pull out our bag of tricks to get us over to the front door and inside that way. Bradley, can you do your mindchime to keep our sounds from projecting? And who can blind any neighbors to our presence?"

Both Matt and Jake signaled they had an ability close to that. "We call it mindunwind, which really means they become momentarily confused and disoriented, allowing us to slip past." Jake explained.

"Works for me," I said. "So we use mindchime, mindunwind, and mindgrind to get us up to and in through the front door without the neighbors noticing. You all are weird, by the way. I feel dorky just saying those words, but whatever. Just thought you should know."

A few snickers broke out amongst the remaining teammates, but Charlie's look of disdain quickly dissolved them.

Matt stage-whispered in my ear, pretending he didn't want Charlie to overhear but obviously messing with him, "We gotta get our kicks somehow. Old Charlie's had a stick up his butt for the last century or two. Making up a whole string of rhymes for our abilities is the least of the ways we've devised to torment him."

"Hardy har," I replied. "Wait until I get some good abilities of my own. I'm gonna make up all new nicknames for them, only mine will rhyme with brain instead of mind.

For instance, I could start with a new pet name for you . . . BrainSprain has a certain ring to it, wouldn't you say?"

He grabbed me and tickled, which was so not good given that we were standing at the enemy's front gate, AND I had my hands full with Wrath's chain. I quickly slashed my tethers to the group mind so they wouldn't be privy to my extemporaneously out of control girly thoughts. *Not very leader-like, Bay.*

But damn, I can't even run my fingers through those sexy curls of his, I lamented. I was still a teenage girl, after all, and some days my hormones had hormones. I squirmed out of Matt's reach, dragging Wrath and Charlie with me, although there was a part of me that would have loved nothing more than to sink into that boy's arms and never come up for air. *The dude was totally dreamy.*

"TMI, daughter," Wrath chuffed, in what could best be described as a laugh. I was impressed he knew what TMI meant, though, especially since he'd been feral for the past 18 years. "I heard you thinking it when your mother and I were making googly-eyes at each other the other night," he said smugly. "I'm always happy to add a new word to my vocabulary. And those thoughts? Definitely TMI. Plus, with us connected via this big tether, there's no getting away from each other's deepest desires right now; so reel it in, please, young one."

"Jeez, Dad," I said, chagrined. That's the last thing I needed, my father all up in my beeswax. *Yuk!* "You do you, and I'll do me. Once we get this giant link out from between us, I'm gonna block you out of my thoughts from here to eternity, got it?" He gave a wolfish grin—at least I thought it was a grin, because his teeth were on parade: all 2,770,000 of them.

But how would I know? He is a dog.

Since Smith was our go-to guy for all things mechanical, he was in charge of breaking us in through the front door. He pulled a set of tinker tools from his cargo pants, expertly picking the lock and gaining entry within seconds. We filed in behind him, fanning out to the sides in an effort to protect our flank and each other if need be.

As far as we could tell the place was deserted, and looked like it hadn't been lived in for many moons. Although there was furniture, it was mismatched and grimy—like they got it from the city dump—and dirt and dust coated everything.

We first investigated the room where Matt had been found leaning up against the wall.

There were no cameras to be found, which was weird, and no one got a sense that this was anyone's permanent address. So what could possibly be here that was so important to overthrowing Perrin?

We split up to cover all the rooms, and Charlie and I decided to stay with Wrath. Granted, it was less decision, more necessity, given that we were all still chained together, but it made for a good joke anyway. Unlinking at this moment, even if we could, would be decidedly unwise.

We were our own little team of three.

But at least Wrath's no longer chained in the backyard. That's a start.

The three of us took the basement, because all the super-creepiest stuff happens down there, and we didn't want to miss out on anything bad. You know, 'cause we just couldn't get enough horrendousness. *That's sarcasm, people.*

Plus, our guts were drawing us in that direction. *Just my damn luck.*

We crept down the stairs single file, Wrath in the lead, sniffing and peering around for any signs of danger as he descended. I never liked basements in the first place, but now I had a seriously American Horror Story vibe going on. I mean, who in their right mind wanted to go underground to do their laundry, anyway?

The light was dim, and elicited from a single overhead bulb and two small windows that looked like they'd been broken and replaced recently. The glass wasn't dirty.

That didn't bode well. Had someone broken in to look for something or to stash something? A scritch scritch sound interrupted my panic attack. "Did you hear that, guys?" I asked the others.

"Shhh" Charlie replied. "Of course we are perfectly capable of hearing the same sounds you do. Now kindly stay silent so we can track it down."

"Sorrr-yyy!" I snarked. *I don't know what's crawled up his britches and died today.*

If he heard me he chose to ignore it, which was fine by me. I wanted to get in and out of this place, and the creep factor was only ratcheting up every second I remained underground.

Scritch. Scritch. *What in the fire and brimstone. Do I even want to know?*

Wrath suddenly wrenched his whole body to the left, put his nose to the ground, and dragged us over to the even-more-dimly-lit corner. I was terrified to discover the source of the sound. *Please don't let it be a zombie. Please don't let it be a zombie,* I repeated to myself. As if my day hadn't been bad enough already. The undead would about top it off.

Before us, in a recessed cranny, sat an old and rusty cage.

Inside that rusty cage was the source of the scritching that was sure to later star in my nightmares. An ancient and mangy-looking rat peered out at us heedlessly as he continued his half-hearted attempts to dig his way out of the cage holding him—a zombie rat, perhaps?

Regardless of his zombified-or-lack-thereof status, my heart immediately went out to him. *How long has he been down here? When was the last time he had food or water?* And then I looked to his right, and my heart almost beat out of my chest. Sitting next to him was a rabbit—a white rabbit, who, if such a thing were possible, was in even worse shape than the rat.

This rabbit was so skinny I could visibly count every rib. Rabbits are more fragile than most other critters; he wouldn't last long if at all without immediately intervention.

Charlie mindlinked to the folks upstairs, who flashed down to us and reported that they'd found nothing of note yet.

"Guys, we've got to get these animals out of here and taken care of before they die. We can always come back tomorrow to explore more," I implored.

Everyone acquiesced, and it was decided that Smith would carry the cage with the rat and rabbit inside, flashing them directly to our back entry room since neither the cats nor the dogs could get into that area. It would do as a safe zone for these two creatures while we worked to bring them back to health. The rest of us would come in directly behind him, with Charlie bringing the three of us together so we didn't end up arriving separately. With the risk of the King going feral again, that would be ugly for everyone.

Smith grabbed the rickety crate and jerked it off the

ground to flash. As soon as the cage left the ground an alarm sounded, blaring into the room, and red and white siren lights encircled the circumference. It was both blinding and confusing as hell.

"Go, Smith, Go!" yelled Charlie, and Smith immediately zipped himself and his cargo to our property two blocks away. The rest of us frantically looked around the room for the source of the alarm to see if it could be silenced.

Seeing nothing and knowing sticking around could get us killed, Charlie gave the go-ahead for the rest of the team to get out of there ASAP and back to my house.

So much for a clean getaway. *Why would a starving rat and a skeletal rabbit that someone left there to die be the only things in that hellhole to set off an alarm?*

Once again, I was left with more questions than answers.

Chapter 20: Perrinites

We all crowded into the back entry room, which was clearly not big enough for a congregation of this size. We were sardines.

Everyone jostled for position to peer into the cage, while the rat and the rabbit sat calmly, peering back at us. There was something a little off about their state of mind, my gut was telling me—and while I thanked said gut for keeping me in the know, I secretly just wanted it to STFU already. *Couldn't a girl wallow in denial once in awhile?*

I was so not interested in being the savior of the world... any world, including a world I didn't know even existed a week ago.

I snapped myself out of my bout of self-pity, asking Matt to go to the kitchen and bring back some water as well as some cut up fruits and veggies. The animals needed nutrition now above all else, and Mom would kill me if I didn't immediately care for their physical needs before assessing their mental state after captivity and starvation.

I wished she was here, because she would totally take over the animal ministrations—even shove everyone else out of the way in order to do so—but it was just as well she wasn't home yet. This way we could unlink from my father's chain before she came home and panicked, adding to our stress level.

Rebecca, Ruth, Tara, and a healing Daniel all soon crowded into the room too, wanting to see what all the hubbub was about.

I need a bigger room for this intervention.

Matt and Jake squeezed by bearing a bowl of fresh cool water and a plate of cut up grapes, tomatoes, carrots, and broccoli. I thanked them and held the cage door open while they placed the crunchies inside.

The rat and rabbit promptly launched themselves at the food, tearing into the fresh offerings like they hadn't eaten in weeks. And they probably hadn't. I was frankly surprised they hadn't taken to feasting on each other, *yuk.*

After they'd cleaned the plate of edibles, they turned to the water and guzzled by turn, until the bowl was bone dry. Matt fetched another round of water, and my heart went out to them for their obvious suffering.

While they finished up their meal, Charlie and I turned our attention to the chain and our ongoing and unwilling connection to Wrath.

What to do, what to do?

I first tested the possibility of separating myself from the links. I pulled my left hand back, and it made a suction noise and then popped off the chain. Relief! We weren't stuck together for all of eternity at least. I didn't dare take my right hand off, yet, because that would leave Charlie as the only one attached to Wrath. None of us wanted to go there in a crowded room swimming with edible targets.

Charlie then repeated the experiment, removing one of his hands from the chain, and met with the same suction sound and pop to freedom.

Ok. So we can get our hands off the chain. But how to do it at the same time so that just one of us isn't left connected to Wrath's mind?

And, how do we remove the chain from Wrath for good?

Smith was busy studying the chain. He touched it to see if it would attach to him as it had to Charlie and me, but nothing happened. That was positive.

Then he examined the way it wrapped around Wrath's neck.

There's where we ran into our greatest challenge. The chain melded to one of those electronic collars scientists use to track wolves, and Wrath had told us he remembered a lot of pain when they put it on him. Although, as he'd been in feral state and may not have understood what was happening, the pain could have come instead from the chain connecting to the device we'd left in the backyard. That remained to be seen.

Smith studied the collar for about fifteen minutes, while Wrath lay on a rug and snoozed—like a normal dog—for the first time in 18 years. It was kinda pitiful to watch. He really needed a bath, too. The smell was excruciating and exacerbated by the closeness of the tiny room, but I figured I'd leave that up to Mom when she got home. There was only so much Dad-weirdness I could handle right now.

Smith finally believed he had the right tools and approach for the dismantling job. Our plan was for him to remove the collar from Wrath first, while Charlie and I continued to hold onto our little pieces of the tether. Theoretically, once Wrath was free of the collar and chain, we could drop it without the danger of Wrath (and us) going cray cray.

Fingers crossed.

One immediate concern was that Wrath could or would be tracked here, so we needed that collar off and out the door as quickly as possible. The highway wasn't too far away. Smith and Bradley would flash over there and toss it into the back of a long-distance semi, in hopes that the trucker would drive all night and lead the enemy far astray from our front door.

I still didn't feel comfortable, though. We were way too close to that hell-hole, and now we were in possession of three animals that someone, some cruel bastage, had left there to die.

Did they know that Wrath was not "just a dog"? Surely. So then what was the deal with the rat and the rabbit? I was frustrated by the lack of information.

Smith fiddled with the collar, using tiny screwdrivers and other manly devices that were above my pay grade. But he was badass, I'd give him that. Within the space of five minutes he had the tracker off, and my father was FREE!

Finally wholly and completely LIBERATED! For the first time in 18 years. *Wow.*

Wrath looked around in confusion, and Charlie and I quickly popped the chain off our remaining hand, just in case he was fixin' to go back into feral mind again. Immediately after we dropped our anchor and reached out with our mind tethers, the King's face cleared.

"Dad! Are you ok?" I asked, concerned. We were so close to getting him back, for good; I couldn't let that slip away.

"Yes, Baylee, thank you. I think the confusion came more from the release of the thrall from the chain and collar than from my feral mindstate." He stood and shook himself. "I'm actually feeling clearer in my head than I have in years!"

He had a gleam of intelligence in his eyes that I hadn't seen before.

"I feel so ALIVE, so like the old me," he exclaimed. "In fact, I feel like I could try changing back into human form. Do you think it might work, Charles?"

We hadn't even crossed the bridge yet with the curse and the subsequent turning of him and his warriors into their feral dog forms—for what was supposed to be all of eternity.

And now the King wanted to jump ahead ten steps.

But, really, who could blame him?

We'd first focused on removing his chain from its anchor, and then removing the chain from his neck. With the success of those two ventures behind us, it was reasonable and expected that the King would wonder if it was possible to now overcome the curse.

If we could indeed break the King free from his damnation, then we could break his warriors free when we found them, too.

Charlie pondered for a minute. "Why don't we open up a channel with Perrin, and create a closed session with Mara and Shanti? They will be elated to know you're alive, and might have some insight into why your whole team was affected—and how we can attempt removal of the curse."

"Good idea," Randulf replied enthusiastically. I was so confused over what to call him…he still looked like Wrath to me, but inside he was now himself, Randulf, and he was also my father. And the King of Perrin. *Dilemmas.*

Since Charlie and I had to remain tethered to the King through mindlink to keep him from feral state—or at least we assumed we did—the three of us would create a closed connection to Perrin and all be in on "the call" together.

Charlie handled getting through to Perrin since I was a newby, and I simply hung around in their minds, observing and learning.

It appeared he used a unique version of the mindlink tether to contact them. To my mind's eye, it was certainly nowhere near the size or appearance of the real-life chain that was attached to Wrath, but it was longer and thicker than the mental tethers I'd observed and used between the team. It was also red, which I made note of. That would be easy to differentiate, then, given that the ones between me and the team, and even my father, were silver.

Red, home base on Perrin; silver, teammates on earth. Check.

Shanti was the first to be heard through the link. "Randulf? Is that really you? I had a vision of you yesterday, but was afraid to get everyone's hopes up here on Perrin! I'm so thrilled they've found you and you're safe. How did you come back into your right mind?"

The tone of his reply held a warmth I hadn't heard yet, and I got a little jealous on Mom's behalf. "Shanti, you have no idea how good it is to hear your voice again. We thought our goodbye was final the last we spoke, did we not? Yet fate has handed us another chance to save our dimension, so let's make the most of it. There is so much to tell, and I'd love to have a long conversation with you and Mara soon, but first we need to undertake a brainstorming session with Charles and my daughter, Baylee, who we believe is the prophesied one. Can you confirm?"

Just then the sorceress, Mara, came through the link. "Randulf! Oh my God! We've been so worried—about Charlie, about you, about your team. Tell us everything."

Shanti cut in. "We'll get to that, Mara, but first, yes, Randulf, I can sense that Baylee is the chosen one, for lack of a better term. Your mission to Earth was a success, in that you created a half-immortal who has a chance of taking on the scion and winning. Your sacrifice on behalf of your people makes you truly a man of honor. Baylee, it is so nice to finally meet you. I will be happy to advise and work with you as much as you'd like as we progress along our path."

"Thank you, Shanti," I said, feeling awkward, and quite frankly, scared shitless. "And Mara, thank you as well. Our most immediate need is to figure out how to bring my father back to his human form and in control of his feral mind. For some reason, and we don't know why, he is only lucid currently when he's in the presence of and tethered to both Charlie and myself. Can you help?"

Charlie took over, Thank Dog, and explained everything in depth to both the prophetess and the sorceress. They, luckily for us, were just as baffled as we were that the combination of Charlie and I worked to bring Wrath back into his Randulf mind.

They theorized that, since Charlie was one of the few on Perrin who had strengths rivaling the King's, and since I was destined to manifest great power as well, we were strong enough together to forcefully pull him out of his wild state.

Made sense to me.

"So, can our combined powers go all the way to bringing the King fully into his immortal form and out of the feral?" I wondered.

Mara answered. "Really, I see no harm in trying. Why don't we all work together. Shanti and I will add our powers through the tether, too, which will give your triad a considerable boost. We will combine energies and focus the united power on a mental image of the King in his full immortal form. As we picture him fully and completely whole again, so mote it be."

Alrighty then. Seems easy enough. At least it's not all on me this time.

Randulf stopped us, a note of sadness slipping into his voice. "I could have never hoped for this day to come, and truth be told, I'm still afraid to hope. When I left Perrin, I knew the odds were good I'd never return—but it was a sacrifice I was glad to make for my people. I know many others would have done the same for me. If we do this and anything goes wrong—if I don't make it through to the other side—please tell Candice I love her, always, and tell my people I did my best. One can never ask more than that."

I had tears in my eyes now, but I was so over whining around and being a victim. I wasn't losing my father again, by gum, and we were making this happen. NOW!

I guess he heard me through the link, because he looked at me with love in those green puppy eyes of his, melting my heart. Charlie even got a little verklempt, I think. "Let's do this," he said.

I poured all my third chakra energy into the tether, knowing in my gut it was the strength I needed to complete this task. I could feel Charlie, Shanti, and Mara in there with me, our combined powers shining a blinding radiance racing through the link and into Wrath's body.

It hit him like a bolt of lightning, tossing his body five feet into the air. His eyes rolled back into his head, and he would have fallen head first to the ground had Daniel and Curtis not been quick enough to jump to his aid and catch him, together. They gently laid him flat out on the rug while we continued to pour our combined strengths through the bond and into his fur-covered body.

I didn't know if this much power could kill him, but no one else seemed concerned about that. So I kept focused on bringing my father back—the father I'd never known but always wanted—and they kept focused on recovering the King who lay trapped inside the body of a dog.

Wrath was seemingly out cold, but then I noticed a pale shimmer surrounding his doggie form. As I watched, fascinated, the shimmer became more pronounced, and his limbs began to shift, one at a time, into the body of a man—a man I could only presume was Randulf.

He was also a naked man, I belatedly realized, quickly turning my back to save myself adding another year onto the therapy tab.

There are not enough shrinks in the world to get me through that trauma, I giggled, relief and elation coursing through my body.

But oh, what we'd done! We'd rescued my father from a life of sheer horror, freed him from a lifelong curse, and given him hope of rescuing his warriors and returning them to their pre-feral human/immortal forms as well.

In that one moment, life was incredible. I grinned.

Someone flashed to grab Randulf a set of clothes, and shortly thereafter a pair of strong arms encircled me. I turned in those arms to see the father I'd dreamed of since a little girl—a strong man with dark hair, an answering grin, and eyes alight with what could only be awe.

I mean, what girl doesn't long for a father who loves her, who sees her, who knows her dark and light, and adores her anyway?

I was overcome with . . . what was that feeling, exactly? I didn't know.

Euphoria? Intoxication?

Oh, this is awkward, falling apart in front of all these people.

But the emotions wouldn't stop coming. I was feeling, dammit—feeling so much love, confusion, joy, and hope—and hating the vulnerability of it all.

Tears streamed unbidden down my cheeks, and my father looked at me with eyes of sorrow and, dare I say it, love.

He took his fingers and lifted my chin, so that I'd be forced to meet his eyes. "I'm so sorry, Baylee. Please believe me that I never wanted to leave you and your mom. I'm grief-stricken that by my actions I've sentenced you to a life of sacrifice as well; at the time I felt it was the only choice for our people's survival.

"I had no idea in the abstract planning phases how wholly I would come to love you and your mother, my family." He gave me a squeeze.

"Rest assured, both my team and Charlie's team—and all the people on Perrin who aren't flushed out as traitors—will proudly fight by your side. We will bring this conspiracy to an end, and then I promise you can have your life back to live as you see fit—either on Perrin or on Earth, in whatever way brings you the most joy."

I offered him a tentative smile and nestled myself into his flannel shirt, wiping my tears and snot as I went. *I have a father. And he loves me. My life might just be complete; impossibly so.*

I had no desire to think about tomorrow.

And then my mother walked through the door.

CHAPTER 21: FAMILY

*W*ell. *Now we have some splainin' to do.*
And, I'll have to share the father I just found with
another woman. Boo.

Most of us were still scrunched together in the back entry
room, while Mom had come in through the garage, flinging
open the door from the living room and peeping inside.
Janie stood behind her, her jaw dropped at the sheer number
of people crammed into the little room.

"What the devil is going on here?" Mom asked, confused
and, if I wasn't mistaken, a little miffed.

"Um, Mom, we have a LOT to tell you . . ." I started. But
then her eyes lit upon my father, still holding me as if he were
frozen in place.

"R-R-Randulf?" More confusion. She sounded lost,
overcome. I recognized the feeling. "Is it really you?" Her
voice was shaky and weak. Janie cradled her, leading her to
the couch and gently pushing her into a sitting position.

My father finally shook himself out of his stupor. He gave
me another quick hug and kiss on the top of my head, and
then rushed out of the room and over to where Mom sat,
in shock for the second time this week. I guess she hadn't
totally believed Dad was actually Wrath, or she thought we'd
never be able to remove the curse, at least not so soon.

Now it was his turn to envelop HER in his arms, and I felt a sharp pinch of jealousy that I'd lost him so quickly. *And to an older woman at that*, I smirked.

But I loved my mom to pieces, even though she drove me batshit most days. She deserved this happiness, WE deserved this happiness, and now I had hope that down the road—after all the ugly was over—we could be an actual family.

It seemed rude to watch Mom and Dad in their intimate moment, but I couldn't seem to look away. I noticed the others were openly staring too, which made us one big creepy family.

Dad held Mom for what seemed like hours. She wept into his shirt, probably combining her snot with mine, and he whispered into her ear. His big, capable hands kept running through her hair, soothing away her pain.

Finally she calmed herself enough to sit back and take a really good look at him. She got a mischievous smirk on her face, and ran her fingers over his lips, across his cheeks, and up through his hair. "Well, at least you didn't bring that gawdawful stench over from your doggie self, honey," she grinned.

"But, methinks someone still might be in need of a shower." She mimed holding her nose, and he tickled her mercilessly in return. I had a feeling they were dropping right back into their old flirtatious banter, and I'd never seen Mom like this before. "Maybe I need to help you out in there?"

Ew. TMI, TMI, TMI!

Dad looked over at me with a big grin on his face. "Get used to it, baby girl. You've missed out on 18 years of being grossed out by your parents. We've got a lot of catching up to do!"

He grabbed Mom, threw her over his shoulder, and raced upstairs with her, dodging curious dogs and astounded Perrinites as he went.

"Well, that was disturbingly awkward, eh?" I announced to no one in particular. There were nods, murmurs, and a weird shuffling about from the crowd.

Charlie was practically apoplectic. "I've never seen the King act playfully before. I guess Candice does bring out the youngster in him. Huh. I shall need a moment to ponder my new reality." He slowly sank himself down onto the couch that the two lovebirds had just vacated.

I threw myself down beside him, cuddling up to him and giving him a big hug. "Don't worry, Charlie, you're still my favorite gay uncle."

He responded woodenly to our new joke, like I hadn't just made a funny. "I'm not gay, dear, not that there's anything wrong with that." The rest of us dissolved into shrieks of merriment, his attempt at being unfunny funnier than if he'd tried to entertain us.

It felt good to laugh. I think we all felt a bit of relief and hope in the moment, and that was nothing to sneeze at after two incredibly tense days.

And, when the King and Mom were done "showering," maybe we could get down to the business of finding out more about the rat and rabbit show we had going on in the entry room.

Always another problem awaits. But I wouldn't allow anything to take away this one moment of bliss.

I earned that much.

CHAPTER 22: DATE

I was still, admittedly, on a bit of a high from having Daddy-O back in my life. At the risk of sounding all foofoocuddlypoops, it was like half of my heart had been missing since birth, but now it had miraculously come along and glued itself back together, pumping out love right alongside the blood. *Sappy, I know.* Yet I hadn't even noticed it was AWOL or that my heart only worked halfway. Freaky.

Bradley and Tara were poring over cookbooks again, trying to figure out what deliciousness they could make for a crowd of this size for dinner. I suggested something simple like vegan sloppy joes and French fries—I knew we had the ingredients for that—but they looked at me askance and threw me out of the kitchen.

"Geez, just trying to be helpful," I muttered, making my way over to Matt. Maybe a little harmless flirting would give me an outlet for all the extra heart chakra energy I was suddenly saddled with.

I felt the tentacle of his tether trying to hook up with mine through the mindlink, but I playfully slapped it away. "Not on the first date, buddy," I winked.

"Oooh, first date?" he sidled up to me. "I like the sound of that! Seriously, do you want to escape this place and go grab something to eat at the local pizza joint? I would so love to catch a minute of freedom and downtime with you…and, indulge in a slice of the pie while I'm doing it." He rubbed his tummy excitedly, hunger for both me and the idea of pizza lighting his eyes.

My high, so rudely trounced upon by Bradley and Tara, raised its head and gave a saucy nod. "Oh, Hells to the Yeah!" I beamed, "Let me go change, then, be back in a sec." I gave him a look that I hoped said, "You're gonna change too, right? Nerdy dad sweat pants doth not date material make."

"Readin' ya loud and clear, Sarge," he said, giving me a salute and flashing himself up to the attic to steal more of my father's clothes. *Gah, I hope there's something there that doesn't look too early 1800's.* I cracked myself up. *And, note to self: if you're gonna flirt with Matt, and maybe even, gasp, date him, make him buy new clothes first.*

I sensed a trip to the store might be in order after our lightly flirtatious dinner.

I gleefully grabbed some goth attire that I usually didn't get to wear around my mom, even digging out netted gloves and my black-knit hat. I paired them with black skinny jeans and a deep red tank with a ripped little black number overtop. I grabbed my faux leather jacket and my fake Martin's and gave myself a final check in the mirror, thinking I didn't clean up too bad after all.

I hope there's no one I know from school there. I really wanted to be incognito tonight, and just enjoy getting to know Matt as a human. Err, immortal. Whatever.

I hadn't been on a date in over a year, ever since things ended so badly with Rick, aka he-who-shall-not-be-thought-of-ever-again. *Shudder.* I was violating my own rules. *Not tonight.*

I found my wallet and car keys on the dresser, and flashed back downstairs to meet up with Matt. I could get used to this flashing business, but I realized I was gonna have to be careful I didn't do it while we were in public without thinking. It was becoming second nature to me to use it whenever possible at home, especially because of the gates at the top and bottom of the stairs. It was annoying to open and close them all the time to keep the cat maniacs and dog maniacs separate and alive. This way I could just bypass all that. *So convenient.*

I suspected Dad would be filling Mom in on everything anyway, on an as-needed basis, so I could be relaxed enough to be my new self—whoever that turned out to be—at home, anyway.

Matt was looking on the hot side himself, and must have jumped in the shower. *Don't think about that hunka hunka in the shower, Bay.* There was way too much sexy goodness in that thought; but then the mental image of Matt in the shower slowly morphed to another of my mom and dad in the shower, and the horror of it all killed the moment.

Ew. Sexy showering fantasies ruined for life—thanks, Mom and Dad.

Matt had found some acceptable jeans that didn't look too last century and a polo shirt. Well, he certainly wasn't my emo-match made in heaven, but at least the sweats were gone. I'd take it.

His shoulder-length dark curls were still wet from the shower, he'd shaved his five o'clock shadow and gotten ahold of some cologne. *Damn, he fills out that polo nicely,* I thought, eyes wandering into places they had no business being. He gave me a big grin and waggled his eyebrows. "Do I pass inspection, your Highness?"

"You'll do, sailor," I flirted, grabbing his hand and heading toward the door.

"We'll be back in a couple hours, everyone," I yelled behind me. "Don't interrogate the rat and the bunny rabbit until we get back. And no torture!" That got a few chuckles. *Tough crowd.*

"Enjoy your hot date!" Jake teased, giving us a wave. "Don't do anything I wouldn't do."

"Ha," Curtis shot back. "The sky's the limit, then, Baylee. Rworrl!" he exclaimed, pawing the air with his hand and mimicking a cat in heat. *Disturbing.*

Oi. I could see I was never gonna live this date down. But the love and camaraderie so obviously shared by this group gave me another warm fuzzy moment in a day chock full of them already. *My heart can't take much more of this feel-good crap!*

I wasn't gonna lie, though; I liked it, and the feeling of belonging.

I pulled my little champagne-colored Saturn out of the garage, and Matt watched in fascination as I drove away, memorizing every move. Did they even have cars on Perrin? I didn't know, but figured I'd bombard him with questions while we ate.

We chose Mama's Pizza, because I had a major hankering for their grilled Veggie sub (it was totally the best in town), and it was easy to make vegan so I could cut through the guilt. Matt was dying to try real Italian pizza since he'd been eating solely as a cat for the past year, and I kinda envied his wide-eyed wonder as he slowly and deliberately chewed that first slice.

I wondered if I'd be so in awe of the cool stuff Perrin had

to offer.

"Oh…My…Goddess…." he slurped with enthusiasm. Each bite was met with such gusto that I thought he was actually going to start purring. *I wouldn't mind getting a look at that.*

Once he got himself under control, and half of his pizza devoured, we started delving into our pasts. His seemed much more interesting than mine, but he also acted enthralled by my life. *I guess when you're from another dimension, flushing a toilet here on Earth might seem kinda exciting.*

He shared with me stories of himself and his people, and I felt like I was actually getting to know the real Matt, instead of the smiling and flirtatious one seen on the surface. We'd taken a booth way at the back in an alcove, far out of range of anyone else in the place, and so could talk freely about our histories without fear of being overheard.

I was most curious about what Perrin was like, and how old Matt actually was, despite looking to be in his early-twenties at the most.

Matt sat back, taking a break after his fifth slice. "Well, I've been around for about 500 Earth years. We could be called immortal by Earth standards, which would lead humans to refer to us as gods—but we as a general rule don't like or use that term anymore. When we thought of ourselves as godlike, we played around in things on Earth we had no business sticking our noses into. Since that time we've evolved to referencing ourselves as merely long-lived beings, which we hope keeps our egos in check a little better."

I was fascinated.

He continued. "However, there is a minority on Perrin who fights that, who still wants us to be seen as gods, extend our reign, and rule the humans here on Earth. They're all about power and control, like most despots, and their rule would not be humane. I suspect such a group is behind the disturbing events which have taken place here, from the birth of the scion to the imprisonment of the King and his warriors, although I don't have all the details worked out yet."

I curled my lip in frustration. "How can we find out more? We need to capture one of these ninjas and question him or her," I blurted, thinking aloud.

"Good idea," he said, "but first let's see if we can get anything out of the rat and rabbit. We think they might be Perrinite, and were just too unhealthy initially for us to sense them as immortals. But now that they've have access to food and water, their natural healing is kicking in. We'll see for sure when we get back."

"Dang, that would be cool! I never even considered that, but it would make sense, and would explain why they were seen as valuable enough to set off an alarm." I wrinkled my brow in thought. "So, can Perrinites die if they are immortal?"

"Well, yes and no. We can die if the trauma is too vast and hits us all at once, but then our souls recycle back into a new body, unless we choose otherwise. Starvation and thirst won't normally kill us, although we can appear to be in very bad shape like Wrath and the animals we just found. Many of us spend about 750-1000 years in one body, and then willingly leave and return in the body of a newborn. We don't have many babies on Perrin, but when we do they are planned for and volunteered for occupancy by older Perrinites who wish to start over."

"Incredible!" I said, excitement bringing me to the edge of my chair. "One more question: will the age difference between Mom and Dad be obvious now? I've been worrying about that, since everyone but Charlie looks to be early-mid twenties in age. I would think Mom would be freaked out that Dad appears so much younger than her. I know I would be if I were her. That won't be good for their relationship."

"The King has more abilities than anyone on Perrin, so I'm sure he can just age progress if he wishes to. We can all vary our age to some extent, and there are those in our realm who willingly age themselves as the years go by, especially if they've found a mate and want to experience growing old together like you do here on earth. I suspect the King will just tweak his age to match Candice's, so you won't have to get too weirded out that your dad could look young enough to be your boyfriend."

Har har.

"Thank the Dogs for that," I muttered. *One worry down.*

Matt explained that twins were fairly common on Perrin, which is why his team had two sets of them. With their advanced genetic engineering, prospective parents could choose to birth one or two children, and many chose two so that their kids would have built-in playmates.

He felt like Jake was more of a best friend than anything, and they hung out together most of the time even when they weren't on a mission. In addition, he also liked to read and play group sports, although both were different there than what we had here in the States.

Matt was beyond excited about exploring the U.S., and couldn't wait to get time to investigate all Earth had to offer; he promised he'd explain to me how any new experiences compared to similar activities on Perrin.

"So, do you all have cars there? I noticed you were

fascinated by all-things-driving on the way here."

"No, not really. We can flash pretty much wherever we want to go as long as it's within a reasonable distance and we're not sick or injured. We just need to be able to visualize it—either from a prior visit or from photos—and we can get ourselves there. So we don't have much need for vehicles like you have here on Earth. But I think they're amazing, I can't wait to drive! I feel like I've been definitely missing out on this Earth invention."

Admittedly, he was adorbs when he looked like a little boy about to get a new toy, but I interrupted, confused. "Is that why you couldn't flash us from the school the other day, because you hadn't been to my house before?"

"No, we could have flashed to somewhere else local just to get us out of there, so that wasn't the challenge. When we found you at the school, we couldn't flash away due to the formaldehyde in our systems. It messed with our strengths for a bit, until we were able to get it worked out of our bloodstreams."

He switched back to my question on cars. "We do have some airplane-like travel methods for long distances, but not really autos. However, after seeing some of Earth's technologies, I'd like to lobby to bring a few ideas back with us—given that we succeed in saving our realm and continue on as a species, of course. You've got some super-exciting stuff here. And that includes pizza!"

With that, he happily dug back in and finished the whole large pie by himself.

I finished my sandwich too, and sat back, oddly happy. I knew that my world was crazy right now, and there was a very real chance I was going to make a huge mess—and maybe even get myself and a whole realm full of people killed.

But, I'd just had a wonderful first date with a hot guy, my father was back, he was still deeply in love with my mother, AND I had insane new powers and strengths I hadn't really even gotten to explore yet.

I was gonna choose to enjoy this moment, because for once all felt right in my world. I smiled.

Chapter 23: Reality X2

I checked in with Mom via text before we left the restaurant, and she said they were just sitting down to dinner themselves. That meant we had time to head to the mall to pick up a few provisions in the gear department for Matt before making our way home to discuss our guests.

I wasn't a shopper myself. I didn't like spending the money, I had no patience for trying on a million outfits to find that one good one, and I hated dragging a bunch of crap home with me that just cluttered up the place.

Amaya was always schlepping me to the mall against my will and making me try stuff on. She had three credit cards and a boatload of gift cards that kept inexplicably finding their way into her hands. I wasn't so lucky. Yeah, Mom and I weren't destitute thanks to the money Dad had left us when he "died," *(no givey-backeys on that)* but we still tried to live within our budget—and that definitely didn't mean a new outfit for either of us every week.

Apparently the same budgetary constraints didn't apply to Amaya, who was always either looking to buy or shopping online and having it shipped to her.

I wished we were the same size, because she regularly tossed clothing aside after only one or two wears, giving whole bags of brand new rejects to her cousin two grades lower than us. But since I was taller and thinner—she wore petites in one size larger than me—we couldn't do the friend swap thing. Bummer. She wasn't missing out but I sure was.

Matt had a good idea of the style he'd feel most comfortable in, but we toured the entire mall once so he could get a quick idea of what each store offered.

I didn't think he'd be into the goth look like me, and he wasn't, but it was ok. I reminded myself that influencing him to buy clothing that turned me on but made him feel awkward or like someone he wasn't wouldn't be cool. I sucked it up and said nice things as he stocked up on more collared polo-style shirts and, well, dad jeans.

Ok, ok, they weren't all the way to dad jeans, but they took a side street in that general direction. I knew he was older than me (way WAY older) but he didn't need to dress it, given that by Earth standards he looked to be pretty close to my age range.

Don't get me wrong, he was HAWT no matter what covered his bod, and he could fill out a polo and a pair of dad jeans like nobody's business. He was still boy-toy eye-candy to me—just more like republican gym guy eye-candy instead of the slinky bad-boy eye-candy I normally zeroed in on.

And, his shoulder length curls and dark bedroom eyes saved him from the absolute gym-dad zone. It was all good.

He bought a few things for his brother too, since they were the same size, but said he didn't want to deprive Jake of the fun of finding his own style, so figured he'd bring him back tomorrow while I was at school.

School! Yikes. He had to go and remind me.

We headed home, arriving just as the gang finished clearing the dinner dishes, talking and laughing and teasing each other (and us, for running off on our "date"). We all grabbed cups of coffee, tea, or hot chocolate and gathered in the living room for a family meeting.

I was surprised and tickled to see that Janie was still there. Apparently she'd been indoctrinated into the club, given the proper clearances, and was handling it like a champ. She was talking and cracking jokes with Ruth, and I wondered if maybe there was a little flirtation going on between the two.

Janie was openly-gay, had been for as long as I'd known her, and I suspected that Ruth (and Rebecca?) could be too. Janie worked a government job that she described as "boring but safe", but in her off-time she was anything but those two descriptors.

Janie was Mom's best friend, and had been a part of my earliest memories, so she must have been hanging around our house forever. She was 39 years young, with short, dark hair and a thin, athletic build that came from daily runs and steadfast gym workouts. She was a wise-ass, always cracking jokes at the expense of whatever crappy politician was trying to take away her rights this week. She was big into marathon running, but loyally skipped the trail on Sundays to hang out with Candice.

She and Mom had decided to take up kayaking last year, and in good weather they'd duck out early with their kayaks and their waterproof Go-Pros, the Thornton River firmly in their sights. They'd drag back to the house hours later, exhausted, wet, and giggling like schoolgirls about whatever spills and mishaps they'd experienced that day.

To my knowledge, Janie's romantic relationships had been few and far between, and her exes were frequent fodder for her crazy sense of humor. I'd be thrilled if she found someone who made her happy—especially now that her current significant other, i.e. Mom, had her man back in her life.

I brought my attention back to the King, aka Dad, aka Randulf, aka the personhood version of Wrath, as he launched the meeting.

"I'd like to officially thank Charlie, his team, and of course my daughter Baylee for rescuing me from my 18-year-hell-on-this-dimension sentence. The only blessing of my purgatory was that I really didn't know any better, and lived in a feral, slathering state as each day bled into the next. I have no memory of what happened, if I killed anyone, or what I was assigned to protect. Now that I can comprehend the agony I endured through sane eyes, I'm truly saddened and appalled that anyone from Perrin would stoop to being this cruel. I fear we are truly not the enlightened society I'd believed we were for so long."

He stopped, rubbing his eyes and slouching, like he bore the weight of the world on his shoulders. "Obviously, it's our job to stop the persons or group behind this plot. From the prophecy, which Charlie has filled you all in on, we know that if we have a chance of halting our approaching destruction, Baylee is destined to play a major role. I, as a new father and the one who set this plan in motion, feel at fault for the load I've hoisted onto her shoulders. I'm sorry, Baylee." He stopped and pulled both Mom and I in close, squeezing us like he never wanted to let go.

I peeked at him from the corner of my eye, and got a little verklempt when I saw the purity of his love reflected back at my mother and myself. The truth was, I didn't blame him for our fate. He'd taken the only chance available to him to save his world, and I was pretty sure I would have done the same.

He'd paid an 18-year price for his sacrifice, some of which I'd witnessed with my own eyes and knew to be horrendous. He'd suffered enough.

Despite all the hardship, Dad was still a handsome man, although I wasn't comfortable with the fact that he looked barely over 25. I hoped that Matt was right; that Dad could age himself older, so he and Mom didn't look messed-up together. I needed to have a discussion with him about that. *ASAP.*

I mean, Mom was an attractive 41, but she was still 41, and—like most moms—would obviously be cradle-robbing if she appeared to be dating a 25-year-old.

Plus, can you imagine all the cougar upkeep needed to compete with the hawt young thangs? *Ugh. NO way! Forgeddaboutit!*

My father was tall, around 6'4", with a corporate-looking hairdo, his brown locks swept back and falling in short layers. I wondered how he came out of 18 years as a dog looking like he just had his hair done yesterday, but I guessed he had his ways. His eyes were gorgeously green, and if he weren't my father I'd probably be drooling over him about now. *Ew.*

I did wish I'd inherited those beautiful green eyes instead of Mom's hazel set. *Just my luck.*

Mom broke in. She was not one for mincing words, so I shuddered to think what was going to come out of her mouth now that it was confirmed her daughter's safety would be at risk. She held tight to Dad, but stood taller and cast those hazel eyes around the room, daring anyone to take her on.

"I've had a little time to come to grips with the reality of our situation, and I have to say I'm struggling here. To hear that my daughter is half immortal, and—lest we forget—

her father is from another realm and was never the man I believed he was? Was never the man I fell in love with?" Her voice rose in pitch. *Uh oh.* I recognized that tell. *Things are about to get ugly.*

"Oh…and that he somehow turned into a feral dog and ended up chained right near me for the last five years, AND now I'm expected to just give up my only child to the lot of you, who will put her in mortal danger while I stand helplessly by and do nothing? Does that about sum it up?"

A tear streaked down her face, and her voice quieted. The group hung their heads like our dogs when she lectured them about their latest destructive adventure.

"For the past almost 18 years it's been just Baylee and I. Randulf was missing, and I had to suck it up and be both mother and father to our daughter. I had to find a way to make ends meet even when it seemed impossible, to work and raise our girl, to love her and feed her and clothe her. Now you want to take her away on a dangerous mission, and I'm supposed to just get over it. Well, it's not working. I'm not getting over it very well."

I stepped away from Dad and pulled Mom to me, hugging her close. "Believe me, Mom, I'm scared too. I feel like all these years you've been the leader, the strong one, and suddenly that has flipped and I'm supposed to be the capable one. But I'm not ready. I've only had a little more time than you to process what this means for me, for us, for the world. I don't like it any more than you do, but the bottom line is that if I don't do it, their realm dies. Maybe ours does too.

"The bad guys, whoever they are, seem intent on ruling the earth as gods, while we submit to their every whim. That's not a life I want, and I know you wouldn't want that either." I stopped and pulled in a deep breath.

"All these terrifying truths leaves me with only one tenable path. I have to do this. I have to learn to fight, learn to harness my powers, and lead this team and whoever else we can find into battle. I'm scared, I'm terrified, I'm devastated. But at the same time, I'm 'the one.' So I don't get the luxury of screwing over the world because I'm scared. Neither do you.

"I want nothing more than to lay in bed with BooBoo and Khronos, and however many other four-legged critters I can drag in, and get lost in a good book. I want to pretend all this ugly doesn't exist, that people are really good when given the chance instead of power-hungry monsters. But our reality doesn't show that right now; our reality says these monsters exist and they are coming for us.

"Maybe if I stand and fight, we can have the reality of our dreams back. Which leaves me with only one choice: become a warrior, and fight like hell to protect both our worlds."

A shout went up around the room, as my team members started to sense the passion I felt welling up inside of me. I had no idea when, I had no idea how, and I had no idea if I could or would succeed. What I did know is that I wasn't going down without a fight.

And training started now.

CHAPTER 24: PRISONERS

The mood in the room turned somber yet determined, as we discussed how best to move forward. It was decided we should bring our guests, aka the rat and the rabbit, into the living room where we had enough space to shift them into their immortal forms so we could question them.

The dogs posed a problem with this plan, given that most of them were prey-driven and the site and smell of a rat and a rabbit was already getting them worked up through the door of the entry room. There was no way we could safely work with them while the dogs breathed down our necks and theirs.

We decided to move their crates into Mom's office and give them kongs with peanut butter to keep them occupied; then hope against hope they'd fall asleep with nice full bellies. A sleeping dog was a well-behaved dog, after all.

While Mom, Janie, Rebecca, and Ruth got the dogs out to pee and settled in their crates, Matt and I prepared more food and water for the rat and rabbit. Everyone else spread out around the room and waited for go-time.

When everyone was situated and relatively quiet, Smith brought the cage with our guests out into the living room, humming soothingly to them as he walked. He appeared to be getting a little attached to them, given that he was the one who'd physically rescued them, hovered over them while they ate and drank, and watched for signs they were coming back to health. It was kinda sweet.

Already they were markedly improved from when we first saw them, and I agreed with Matt that they had to be immortal to be able to bounce back that quickly. I was trying to sense the "otherness" of them that Matt had sensed, but I wasn't yet able to pick up on anything. I was disappointed, but reassured myself that I'd get better with time. It'd only been two days since I'd found out Perrin existed and that I was half immortal, so expecting myself to be super-teen in that amount of time was a bit presumptuous.

I removed my mind from ME and focused on our guests.

Charlie, who was used to being the lead interrogator on Perrin, started off. He spoke aloud, and was gentle about it, presuming that—given that these two were imprisoned and in awful shape—they were indeed our allies and not the enemy.

"Good evening Rat, Rabbit. I trust you are feeling a bit better now that you've had nourishment. Let me get right to the point. We know that you are Perrinite; we can sense you, as I assume you can sense us. We need you to either switch back to your immortal forms so we can talk, or open up a mindlink with me. Are you able to do that?"

We waited. Nothing.

I looked at him enquiringly, wondering if I was missing something. He shook his head.

He tried one more time. "Rat, Rabbit. If you can understand me, I need you to send out a communication link."

I had a thought, and quickly opened up a channel from

me to Charlie. "Hey, Charlie, what if we, together, can bring them around the way we did Dad? Surely we have this mindmeld skillset for a reason. Let's put it to use."

Dad nodded approvingly. He must have been slinking around in our link without me noticing. *Sneaky bastage. He must be a mindlinkslinker. Lol.*

Charlie and I hooked up our tethers the way we'd done for Wrath, and focused our considerable power—which I was beginning to get a better grasp on—toward the consciousness of the rat. We blasted through what felt like a firm concrete wall in his mind, and immediately were overcome by an immense sense of relief, a grasping for our tether with a frail and diffident one of his own.

We dialed our powers back to low and calmly accepted the link, trying to soothe the rat, whose confusion and agitation were apparent to us now.

"Hello," Charlie said gently. "Do you know where you are, who you are? Do you remember how you got here?"

The slight brown rat lifted his nose, sniffing the air. "How do you do, sir, madam. I recognize you, Charles, as the King's lead investigator. And King, how lovely to make your acquaintance. I'm so pleased that you've been found safe and sound." He nodded in the King's direction. He'd apparently sensed the King in his head, although I hadn't yet been able to. *I have some work to do.*

The King gave a rueful smile of acknowledgement that he'd been caught, and nodded at the rat. "Well done, Krupert. Not many can catch me slinking around in their minds, very impressive."

Krupert? Never heard that name before.

He raised himself up at the King's praise. "Well, sir, when

you excavate and explore tunnels for a living, you get used to noticing every little nuance and sensing presences that others cannot. Most would not see you there lurking, and it seems your own daughter cannot yet do so, although I do understand she's only had her powers for two days." He then looked at me and continued mildly.

"And yes, young lady, Krupert at your service. My parents combined their names a la American tradition today, although this was done hundreds of years ago—I guess they were ahead of their time. Her name was Kryan and his was Rupert, so I became Krupert. Admittedly, it has to grow on you."

I giggled at his longsuffering attitude couched in a tongue-in-cheek sense of humor. *I think I'm gonna like Krupert after all.*

"I have a mind block around what happened, but I will try to ferret my way around it in the next couple hours, now that I'm back in my right mind. I can tell you that I was kidnapped from Perrin as I was exploring a tunnel about a year ago. I am the leader of my rat pack there, and I came upon some interesting anomalies in my explorations. I intended to bring my findings to the leadership of the realm, but someone double-crossed me and next thing I knew I was stuffed in a sack and poofed to Earth. That's the last I remember at this moment. I'd like to request a little time to remember more."

"Request granted," sighed the King. "Charlie, why don't you and Baylee bring around the rabbit, and see if we run into the same proverbial wall, while Krupert takes some time to think."

Krupert climbed out of the cage and up onto the couch, where he curled up next to Smith. Judging by his happy grin, Smith seemed tickled that he was chosen by the small rat. Maybe Krupert felt a similar affection for Smith as his rescuer, even if he didn't realize why just yet.

Next we tackled the rabbit. *Not literally, of course, that would be wrong.* Charlie and I combined our tethered energy and blasted through a similar wall in the creature's mind, this one feeling more like wood as it splintered and shattered. Again we felt an instant sigh of relief, and a shy tether reaching for ours. These folks must have really been abused to be so tentative when help finally showed up.

Charlie began. "Rabbit, do you remember how you got here, your name, anything?"

The rabbit recoiled from Charlie's voice in his head, physically pressing himself against the back corner of the cage. His voice was no more than a whisper in my mind. This one was definitely more traumatized than the rat had been.

"Wh-where am I?" he asked.

"You're on Earth, in a state called Virginia in the United States," Charlie educated patiently. He seemed to grasp the fragile mental state of the rabbit. "Can you recall anything about how you got here?" he asked again.

The rabbit settled down a bit, for the moment at least. "My name is Merle. I'm from a Perrin clan of blue tortoiseshell shifters. We work and live in the tunnel system on Perrin, and I started to hear rumors that a portion of the tunnels had been closed off from both the rats and ourselves. Some of our clan members started to disappear, one by one, so I went to investigate. As I was running down some clues, I was grabbed from behind, and the next thing I remember I was starving and so very thirsty, and in a cage with a rat. Then I blanked out again, and now I'm here with you all. Who are you anyway?" His voice became stronger and bolder as he spoke.

He peered around the room, looking into each face one by one, as if memorizing them or searching for memories of some thing, some one. Suddenly his eyes lit on the King, and he did a double take. "Your Majesty! We thought you'd been dead these many years! I'm so grateful to see you're alive. Maybe you can help us now. I believe there is a plot afoot against our people and our realm. But now that you're here, maybe you can set this straight." He slumped back with relief.

The presence of the King had done all we couldn't do to empower him to trust us.

I stepped up. There was no time like the here and now for me to embody my role as champion of the people. I used my gentlest voice so as not to scare him further. "Hello, Merle. I'm Baylee, the King's biological daughter and half Perrinite, half human. We have reason to believe I'm the girl spoken of in the prophecy who is slated to take on the scion in your realm. I have much to learn and we'd greatly appreciate your input. We really need to understand what we're up against. Can you please tell us all you know or remember? And, are you able to turn back into your human form so the whole group can hear what you have to say, too?"

He looked askance at me. I could see I was off to a great start. "This is Charlie, the King's lead investigator, and his team. I promise you they are trustworthy, as am I. And the other two present in the room are my mother and her best friend, both humans who've been roped into our world."

He reluctantly peeled himself off the cage wall and leapt out the open door. Once he was out of the cage and onto the floor, he took a couple hops, and in the blink of an eye turned himself into a gaunt young man with multi-colored hair—the same color his fur had been. Everywhere.

Did I mention he was a very naked young man?

Oi. Awkwardidity. I guess I'd better woman up and get used to seeing an untold amount of guyly bits. How awful for me. I stifled a giggle.

Matt yanked out the clothes he'd bought for Jake and quickly handed an outfit over to Merle. It was a little big on him since his build was slighter, but it worked. He pulled out the remaining set, giving Jake a rueful shrug as if to say, "Sorry, dude, No Soup for You."

Krupert stood, stretched, and hopped off the couch, performing a leap and twirl in mid-air. *He cracks me up.* Then he rebounded and stood before us as a man with the appearance of a forty year old, complete with shaggy brown hair and large front teeth. Thankfully he'd thought to give himself the illusion of clothing, but took Matt's offering and was soon able to drop the charade.

Huh. I know this is shallow, but he's the first Perrinite I've seen that isn't blindingly good-looking. Something told me he'd deliberately aged himself and taken his looks down a notch too. He probably wanted to appear older to be more respected as leader of his rat clan.

With Krupert and Merle back in their manly forms, Bradley hurried to get them some food, while Tara checked them out physically for any wounds or concerns. Although they were both underweight and appeared sickly, she felt sure they'd bounce back to 100% in no time.

Must be nice to be immortal. I wonder if I am too?

I had many questions that only time would bring answers to, and my immortality or lack thereof would be at the top of the list.

Krupert and Merle shook hands, eyeing each other warily. "Do you two know each other?" I asked.

The men stopped sizing each other up and turned to me. "Yes, we do," said Krupert, stiffly. "In Perrin our tribes are in constant competition, since we all live and work in the tunnels. Rabbits and rats handle our affairs differently, so it would make sense that we'd come into conflict over the right way to handle our underground system.

"However, since we're stuck here together, and obviously have both been kidnapped, it would be to our benefit to put aside our differences for the good of our realm, at least until we've managed to conquer whatever woe betides us. What say you, Merle?"

Merle scratched his chin timidly, but his voice was much more forceful than before. "I agree to these terms, Krupert, Leader of the Rat Clan. However, I would like to request that after this is all over, we come to an agreement to divvy up the tunnel system in a fair and balanced manner, so we aren't coming into constant conflict any longer.

"I admit that our people have accused your clan of killing or kidnapping our rabbits, and there have been a lot of hard feelings. Now I understand that we are probably both victims of the same insidious forces. We have much to work through as a people to come back to a place of trust once this immediate threat is vanquished."

Krupert grinned and offered his hand again. "Agreed. I'll enjoy working through our differences. It would make daily life better for all the rat and rabbit folks."

Wow! That was kinda sweet.

Conflict resolution at its finest, and I really didn't have to lift a finger to help it along. I guess in times of need, even enemies can learn to work together for the good of the whole.

The men sat down together and enjoyed their leftovers, gobbling like they hadn't had a decent meal in months—which I guess they hadn't. They reminded me of watching Wrath wolf down his food on the chain, and I was enveloped in sadness all over again. Whoever was behind this plot was really starting to piss me off, and I had a feeling I hadn't yet seen the half of it.

The rest of us made small talk while they ate, discussing and discarding ideas for our next move in this nefarious game.

Mom reminded me that I had school tomorrow, and wouldn't hear of me skipping. I had learned a long time ago that there was no point in begging her about it; and besides, it wouldn't be seemly for the warrior princess to be seen crying because Mommy wouldn't let her off school.

Just as well, I supposed; maybe they'd be able to get more info out of Krupert and Merle while I was at school, and I could just reap the fruits of their labors.

It was well after 10 p.m. now, and I had to be up at 6 a.m. for school. I said my goodnights and showed off my flashing ability for Mom and Janie. At least maybe somebody'd be impressed.

I decided to just shower in the morning, and was grateful that Mom and Dad would make sleeping arrangements for the crew, while I looked after #1. I jumped into my warmest jammies and gathered up BooBoo, Khronos, and whatever other cats I could lure to my bed. The more the warmer, I always said, and in the depths of winter, I'd take all the warmth I could get.

Tomorrow was another day; was it wrong of me to already dread what that day would bring?

Chapter 25: School

I dragged myself out of bed at 6:00 a.m., bleary-eyed and grumbly. Where had my beddy-bye time gone? I felt like I'd had no sleep at all, and yet I didn't remember waking even once, so I must have slept like a log. Maybe Charlie had put me in a mindbind like he'd done to Mom the other night.

I hoped not. I didn't like the thought of anyone messing with my mind again. *Shudder.*

After a long shower I was a little more awake and ready to face the day's challenges. I wasn't looking forward to seeing Amaya, though.

I'd blown her off all weekend, texting her a couple of times each day just to let her know I was alive and that the "relatives" were still in town. I was damn lucky she hadn't shown up on my doorstep.

I knew I didn't have much time before that happened, and I made a mental note to talk to Charlie about bringing her in on the game so I had my best friend to talk to. After all, Janie was "in," why couldn't Amaya be too?

When I flashed down for breakfast, the gang was already up and assembled, with Tara and Bradley whipping up some Vegg and sourdough toast. While I thought they were all insane for being up at the ass crack of dawn without a damn fine reason, I bellied up to the food bar and helped myself to a large fruit salad, toast, and a dish of Vegg.

"Yum," I exclaimed loudly and appreciatively. "Where have you people been all my life? You mean I could have had a nice warm breakfast every day instead of that oh-so-tasty apple my mom left me each morning?"

I snorted as Mom playfully shoved me and ruffled my hair. "I give you hot chocolate, too, don't forget!" she protested. That got a few chuckles from the gang.

Dad insisted he was driving me to school. Mom normally wouldn't let me take my car, because she said the school was only four blocks away and the walk would do me good. But, due to the currently faceless and nameless enemy we were facing, the decision was made that Dad would drive me in my car and then pick me up at the end of the day.

I tried not to feel warm and fuzzy about it, but failed. *Fine, let him be a dad. He's got a lot of making up to do anyway,* I kvetched to myself.

"And get outta my head, Dad," I said, catching him in there for the first time, as I sensed a slight shadow lurking around the edges.

He grinned, proud of me for catching him, and patted my head. I grabbed my backpack, said goodbye to my newly expanded family, and we were out the door.

Once the King and I were alone, his mood turned serious. "Baylee, I'm worried about you today. We have no idea what we're up against, but we have to assume the worst and be on guard constantly. I'm thinking about enrolling one of the team to your school for protection. Shall I send Matt? You two seem to be hitting it off pretty well." He turned more playful, poking me from his side of the car. "Wink wink, nudge nudge."

I rolled my eyes, finally getting to apply standard teenage moves on my dad, something I never thought I'd get to do.

"Drop it, Pops. But yes, if you must send someone, I'd be happiest if it were Matt, then I'd have someone close enough if I needed to mindlink or run into any trouble. And, he's my favorite eye candy, too." I gave him an exaggerated wink and then stuck my tongue out at him.

"Ok, Pumpkin," he said affectionately, giving my hand a squeeze. We'd fallen so easily into a father/daughter camaraderie that it was almost puzzling. I didn't question it, though, because I was grateful to have this opportunity to build a relationship with my father. Despite all the ugly that had been going on around me, he was my one bright spot.

Well, maybe Matt too. I blushed.

As we pulled up to the school dropoff point, he reminded me. "You SHOULD be able to link up to me and/or Charlie if you get desperate. It's a bit of a stretch distance-wise, but since we are two of the most powerful mindlinkers on Perrin, and your abilities are growing by the day, I think we can make it happen. Our powers amplify in stressful situations, too, so I'm hopeful if you need us we're but a mindcall away."

He leaned over and gave me a quick peck on top of my head. "Dad, I'm not in grade school, for crap's sake," I mumbled, jumping out of the car and heading into school before he could yell "Make wise choices" after me. That's all I needed.

My weekend had been so insanity-filled that I'd forgotten how it started: so-called zombie cats chasing humans through the school, culminating with fellow students witnessing me and said undead cats engaged in a hallway powwow session.

Double crap. Now I'm the undead cat-whisperer, and I have

to face all these idjits.

I'd hoped in the ensuing chaos the tiny part I'd played in the debacle (as far as they knew, anyway) would have gone unnoticed, but apparently no such luck. As I skulked through the school doorways, conversations stopped and heads turned my way.

Oh, H E Double Hockeysticks.

Luckily for me, Amaya stepped up to take the heat, even though in exchange for her saving me I was about to endure a something fierce tongue-lashing. It remained to be seen which was the better end of the deal.

"Baylee!" she shrieked, grabbing my arm and dragging me toward the chorus room, our go-to hideout during morning emergencies as it was empty this time of day.

She pulled and yapped, which was really quite the skill if you think about it. "I just can't believe you blew me off all weekend. What gives? Did you realize that I had to go to the freaking movies with TORY! Tory!" she hissed in a vehement whisper, as if to emphasize the horror of it all.

Tory was in our extended friends' group, but Amaya and I were mostly team Amaya and Baylee. A team of two. We hung around other people at parties or school stuff, but our weekends were normally reserved for each other before anyone else.

I felt horrible that she was left out of my weekend, and I knew I needed to bring her into my world soon or all Hades would be breaking loose in my best friendship.

The mental image of her knowing the truth made me want to crack up. I wondered if the all-too-difficult-to-shut-up Amaya would actually be rendered speechless for once.

I placated her. "You know I'm sorry, Bestie. I never meant

to leave you hangin'. I had no idea the fam would stick around all weekend, but now it looks like they might be staying in town for a bit. I'm going to talk to them about you coming over for dinner to meet the whole gang later, if that sounds ok to you?"

She grinned, relieved at finally being included. I knew the feeling of being on the outside looking in, and I never wanted her to feel that way because of me. My mom was always lecturing me about believing actions before words. Words were cheap—anyone could say they loved you—but showing up on a daily basis was what mattered in the end.

Goofy, I know, but I took that sentiment to heart, and I never wanted Amaya to feel like I didn't care. I would remedy this situation.

School dragged until third period, when a new student was announced in History class. Matt! My stomach did a little flip and I slouched back into my desk chair, trying to wipe the girlie grin off my face as he nonchalantly wandered into the classroom with a note for the instructor.

His eyes met mine and they lit up, sending more blood rushing to my already flushed cheeks. I threw a quick glance toward the bloodhound, aka Amaya, and knew I was busted. She stared at me with narrowed eyes, deliberately flicking them back and forth between Matt and I, and then sat up tall and simply pointed her index finger at me.

Uh oh. I knew that was our international symbol for "You have some splainin' to do," and the ferociousness of her gesture added "and you're dead meat" to the equation.

Ugh. I linked up with Matt real quick.

"Matt, my best friend Amaya is onto us. I told her you're all my relatives on Dad's side, but with the way we're ogling each other we're doing some serious damage to our alibi."

"Leave it to me," he countered, up for the challenge.

His eyes quickly found Amaya, and he mega-watted her with a big devil-may-care grin to throw her off the scent. If she thought he merely flirted with all the single ladies, it would buy us some time until I could bring her into the fold.

Plus, she WAS a teenage girl, and not too many could resist a sexy hubba like Matt throwing vibes their way. The ploy worked.

She turned her attention from me to look him up and down, giving her lips an exaggeratedly sexy lick as she did so. *Girl be shameless!* I couldn't stifle a chortle, and knowing she was playing to an audience now, she rolled her eyes dramatically, shifted in her seat, and twisted her hair around her finger. She peeked at Matt from under her lashes to see if she had his full attention.

Yes, she did. The boy stood stock still, mouth agape, at the front of her row like he'd laid eyes on the fairer sex for the first time in his life.

Ok, now I'm getting a little irritated.

"Matt! Jeez, dude, taking the charade a little far, aren't we? Snap out of it and find a seat. Preferably AWAY from my best friend!"

He had the grace to look sheepish at least, grab the first seat he came to at the front of the room, and keep his eyes to himself for the rest of the class.

Amaya smirked, and then turned to me, whispering, "Don't think you're off the hook, girlie. We WILL be having that discussion at lunch. Be there."

Chapter 26: The Lunch Dodge

Luckily Amaya and I had separate fourth period classes, and she didn't have time to grill me between classes because she had to book over to the furthest building for Phys. Ed.

Thanks be to the God of all cows and sheep.

Matt had set up his schedule to reflect mine—something that was sure to feature itself in Amaya's clue widget posthaste—so he caught up and walked with me to Chem lab.

He offered me his best puppy face, knowing I was still ticked off. "I'm sorry, Cutie! Admittedly, I haven't been to Earth in a long, long time, and I'm not used to women who are so blatant with their charms! I think times have changed here. I was struck dumb, that's all. There I was trying to play her, and instead I got played. It was a humbling experience. Can you forgive me?" He touched my elbow, and I couldn't help but look him in the eye.

Argh. He is adorable with those big brown puppy eyes and dark curls. I do want to run my hands through that hair... someday. When I forgive him.

I shrugged, trying to stay mad but failing. "Fine, but she's threatened we're going to have a talk at lunch. To make amends, you have to help me head that off at the pass. We usually eat lunch with Tory and a few other girls. I want you to come eat with us, and be so damn flirty—with everyone, not just me OR Amaya—and fascinating that she forgets all about the grilling of the century she has planned. I can't lie to her again. Can you do that?"

He looked scared; not only did he have to face Amaya so soon after his humiliation, BUT an additional gaggle of fawning adolescent girls, too.

He blanched, but acquiesced.

I had a hard time keeping a straight face. I imagined when he left for his mission from Perrin, the last thing he thought he'd have to fear was being mobbed by a bunch of hormonal teenage girls.

Matt and I made our way to the cafeteria, our reluctance to face the upcoming to-do apparent in our shuffling gait and glum expressions. Luckily we arrived at our table before the others, so I sat Matt two seats to my left, saving Amaya's usual seat to my right. I reasoned that from this distance she could have a front row seat to his eye-candiness, but she'd still be far enough away that she couldn't get too handsy with what I was admittedly viewing as my "property."

I might want to take a look at this new-found possessiveness I've acquired. It ain't raight.

I nodded at Matt in satisfaction with the seating chart, just as Amaya, Tory, and four other girls streamed up, eyes agog at the male model seated in our normally boy-free zone. All conversation ceased and they stopped in their tracks, not knowing where to sit or what to do. I burst out laughing, in disbelief that all it took was one hot guy to stop these chicks' incessant chatter.

Seriously, I've been trying to shut them up for years! And Matt accomplishes it in 3.2 seconds. WTF.

Amaya plopped down to my right, with Tory grabbing the seat next to her, and the others filling in around us. I introduced Matt to the group, explaining that he was a distant relative of my father's, emphasis on the distant.

If we decide to start dating for reals, I don't want anyone thinking I'm slurping on my first cousin, ew!

He launched into a spiel about his family coming in for a visit from Missouri, but just this morning they'd decided they might like to stay awhile after all.

He made sure to introduce himself to and remember each of the girls' names, starting with Tory and working his way around the table, finishing up with Amaya, who he teased mercilessly for playing him this morning when he showed up at class.

"Boy, you look like you do, girls like me gonna be all up in your beeswax!" she flirted; I smiled, doing my best to let it roll off my back. Amaya was seriously the third most important person in my life, so if she wanted to banter with Matt, I was gonna suck it up. Besides, he was doing a great job of getting me through the lunch break without a lecture, and I reminded myself that was the plan after all.

Before we knew it the bell rang for our first afternoon class, and I was officially off the Amaya hook. I breathed a sigh of relief, even though I knew I was just postponing the inevitable.

Matt's voice came through our link. "How'd I do, Princess? Did I meet the high standards of the most beautiful girl in the school?" He gave me a quick smile as we headed off to Phys. Ed.

"You mean my standards for you philandering with other women? Yes, you get an A+," I said wryly.

Matt laughed, and grabbed my hand for a quick squeeze, dropping it when I gave him a dirty look. "Methinks someone has a bit of a jelly belly, eh?"

I scoffed. "Me, jealous? In your dreams, boy. There's a whole school of women you've yet to flirt with, so you'd better get to work; see if I care." I flounced into the girls' locker room and threw on my gym shorts, secretly seething, even though a part of me knew I was being ridiculous.

Um, Bay, you had just ONE date with this guy; now you're all stalker city?

Obviously, I needed to get a handle on myself. It dawned on me that I was sullen because Matt's attention had made me feel special—but what if he really was this way with every girl he meets? What if it wasn't an act? *What if I'm really not special to him after all?*

Go away, evil voice in my head. Special or not special, I still have a job to do. I can't afford to get wrapped up in boys at this juncture anyway.

After all, this was nothing a little volleyball wouldn't fix. I needed to take my aggression out on something, and a net with a bunch of annoying boys on the other side sounded like the perfect solution.

Chapter 27: Shiza Gets Real

As much as I wanted to avoid Amaya setting eyes on Dad, there was no way around it, and he chugged up in my little Saturn to collect Matt and me after school. Amaya, who was still pouting but tagging along with us, let her jaw drop for the second time today.

"Bay, who's the new hottie? How many damn hotties are there in your dad's family? More importantly, why am I not getting to shop in this candy store?" she whispered ferociously in my ear, grabbing me and pulling me to the side.

Ugh. I can't think of Dad that way, please, NO!

"I'll tell you all about it tonight, if I get permission to have you over for dinner. I'll text you in an hour, ok?" I was pleading now, my eyes asking her to give me a raincheck just this one last time.

She dropped my arm in disgust. "Fine. One hour. If you don't text I'm showing up uninvited, so you'd better get this squared away, my friend!"

I gave her a hug and another pleading look, and then jumped in the back seat, letting Matt have the bigger legroom up front.

Dad looked tired and worried, but mustered up a smile for me. "How was your day, kids? Anything go down that I should know about?"

I had no desire to reveal my mile-long jealous streak to my own father, so I let Matt take this one. "Nope, all was good, sir. I was able to get into all the same classes as Baylee, and even got to know her friends a little." He turned and winked at me.

Humph. I stuck my tongue out at him and rolled my eyes. *Brat!*

Then I remembered, dinner with Amaya. "Dad, my best friend knows something's up with me, and she's making life pretty miserable because I can't tell her the truth. Can we bring her in like we did Mom and Janie? I know we can trust her, and if I don't willingly bring her in, I'm going to lose the best friend a girl could ask for." I rushed forward, nervous now. "I told her we'd invite her over for dinner and I'd tell her everything. Please?"

Dad sighed, turning and giving me a brief look. "I'm afraid tonight might be impossible, honey. I have good news and bad news from our work with Krupert and Merle today. We have a lot to discuss when we get home."

I sank back, despair pinging hopelessly from one body part to the next. It seemed that the shiza was about to hit the fan, and I might not have a best friendship left when it was over.

Everyone seemed glum when we walked through the door, a huge difference from the happy mood that prevailed at breakfast this morning. Mom came over and pulled me into her arms, hugging me like she'd refuse to ever let go.

"Oh, Mommy," I whined into her ear, feeling every bit the child I'd been acting all day. There was no doubt my world was seriously off kilter, and I was the first to admit I hadn't responded well. "I had a crappy day too. What in bejeezus is going on around here? Do I even want to know? Wait, I'm starving, give me one sec."

I threw down my backpack and ambled into the kitchen to grab a snack. I knew I was putting off the imminent jolt to the gut that lurked in the living room, but I needed a few minutes to calm down and try to get back to the less grumpy version of myself. The one I used to know.

Matt joined me, and we munched on some corn chips and vegan cheese dip that Bradley'd whipped up in our absence. We didn't talk or flirt after the day's events, but the silence wasn't uncomfortable. Maybe we could be friends after all.

I distracted myself with thoughts of food. Apparently I could add stress eating to my list of faults.

Dang, that's some good dip! I hope I live long enough to eat it again...Yeah, way to decompress, Bay. You're feeling more cheerful already.

Not able to put off the impending doom-athon any longer, we dragged ourselves back into the living room and found a seat on the floor.

Everyone waited, quiet and somber, as if we were at a funeral. It didn't bode well.

When I couldn't take it anymore, I burst out, "Ok, what gives? Why does everyone look like they just lost their favorite kitty, puppy, ratling, or baby bunny in here?"

Eyes shifted uncomfortably, and Charlie took the floor. "Well, while you and Matt were at school, we had some success getting past the mind block in Krupert. The King used his mindslink ability to slip around the edge of the boundary without being detected by whatever is holding it so tightly in place. In doing so, he was able to weaken it enough that, combined with Krupert and myself on the other side, we were able to bust the wall down.

"What came flooding out astounded us all, and we're still trying to wrap our minds around it."

I was on the edge of my seat, now—well, if I actually had a seat…I guess I was on the edge of my floor. I leaned forward.

"Well? The suspense is killing me!"

The King took over. "It's bad, honey. So much worse than any of us knew. Remember when Charlie's team told you about Phoebus, an immoral wretch if ever there was one, who started a Perrinite bloodline with a human woman in 17th Century Europe?"

"Yes, I remember all that. That's why you pulled your people from Earth, hoping the bloodline would die out. Which it obviously hasn't."

"No, it hasn't. When we broke through Krupert's mindwall, we were able to see much of what he'd pieced together before they found him and sealed him up. Phoebus IS the one leading the overthrow of our government, as we all suspected, but it's much bigger than that. His ultimate plan is to overthrow the Earth's government's too, and rule both dimensions—if Perrin survives the upheaval.

"But the truth is, he doesn't much care if Perrin lives or dies…Earth has been his goal all along. Here he can be seen and treated like a god, which is what he's always wanted. Perrin and its people have become more of an unfortunate— and dispensable—fly in the ointment."

The King stopped and leaned over to take a drink of water,

while Charlie continued the meeting without missing a beat. I took a moment to note and appreciate their teamwork and ability to step into each other's shoes as needed.

Mom reached up and pulled Dad down onto the couch beside her, curling into his arms, fear etched on her features and in her body language. My heart quavered. This was indeed worse than anyone had known—now it was both our dimensions in danger, and if we didn't win this war, life as we all knew it was over.

A sobering thought.

I texted Amaya to tell her my mom said tonight wasn't a good night. I knew she'd be hurt and more angry than before, but there was nothing I could do about that right now, with the fate of the world literally resting in our collective hands. I could only hope that I'd be allowed to bring her into my reality as soon as possible, and that once she understood what I was up against she'd forgive me and become a support system. I really needed my best friend back.

"From what we saw in Krupert's mind, Phoebus has been building his own army on Perrin since the second prophecy 20 years ago. He's been recruiting people for a shadow government, promising them power and adulation as gods here on Earth, and staying very well hidden and very much under the radar by building a stronghold concealed in the tunnels that Krupert and Merle manage.

"They discovered an alternative route into the tunnel system, put soundwalls in place, and built closer to the back end; it took years for the rat and rabbit clans to even suspect anything untoward was going on. By the time the clans started quietly investigating last year, it was far too late to put a stop to it. They were outmanned and outgunned.

"Once Krupert and Merle found themselves too close to the headquarters, they were grabbed, interrogated, mindwiped, and thrown in the cage we found them in. We suspect they've been there for six months or more, suffering starvation and thirst but not able to die. In addition to the mindwall and wipe, they soon mentally checked out due to lack of nutrition. They were still alive, but not 'there,' which is the state we found them in."

I was flabbergasted, appalled, disheartened, outraged, and any other four-dollar word you could come up with. What kind of lowlife scum starves and thirsts these animals when they don't even have the solace of death to end the suffering?

These are some sick bastages we're dealing with. I felt the red rage rising from my toes and start up my legs, and I knew working myself into a frenzy right now would not be safe for any of us.

I have to calm down.

I stood and paced the room, finally throwing myself to the ground near Khronos and sticking my face in his fur to reach for something greater than myself, something kinder— because I knew I was fresh out of benevolence.

He gifted me his strength of spirit and filled my love tank with his special brand of puppy cuddles, enabling me to tamp the rage back down into the fiery pit of my soul. That would have to do for now.

I looked up at my peers, who gazed back at me hesitantly. "Go on," I said, impassive now.

Krupert came to the crux of the issue quickly after my meltdown, sensing it was best to get it all out there. "While I was in captivity and before my mind was wiped, they spoke freely in front of me; they felt secure in the knowledge that I wouldn't remember any of it even if I were eventually freed from my prison. I know what the King was sent there to guard."

He had my full attention, now. *This is it.* If we were able to take control of whatever the King had been guarding, we might begin to gain a foothold in this war for planetary control. Right now we were seriously late to the party.

Matt was just as rapt as I, given that he and I were the last to know all things "evil-bad-guy" today. He edged forward, putting himself directly behind me and bracing me with his knees so I had something (or someone) to lean on. Suddenly I didn't feel so alone, and I was grateful he would be by my side, in whatever form that may take.

Reaching the apex of his speech, Krupert finished. "They've spent the last 18 years creating, testing, and perfecting a mind-tether control capable of enslaving every Perrinite in one fell swoop. What was done to your father and his elite guard? Peanuts to what this thing is capable of doing. It's so powerful, and their fear of it falling into the wrong hands— meaning the Perrinite government—so extreme, that they've created five keys or symbols that must work together to power it up.

"Only three people know where all five keys are—their most trusted insiders. At this moment in time, we only know where one of these keys ended up: under the very nose of the man they'd turned against, the man they'd used as their first guinea pig, and the very same man who they most-needed out of the equation for their coup to succeed. King Randulf."

Silence filled the room, as each heart wrestled with the heavy burden we were all being asked to carry.

After a moment of thought, gathering myself and my

pitiful amount of courage into a tightly-wound ball that I could desperately cling onto, I stood resolutely and fired off questions, signaling my willingness to join the mission. "What does the key looks like? Where is it, exactly? And, most importantly, when are we going to get it?"

Chapter 28: The End, or The Beginning?

Over a dozen people jumped up and began blathering at once in a vocal free-for-all until Charlie shouted "Atten-shun!" Perrin's military must have shared some of our protocols, because the whole team, including Merle and Krupert, snapped to attention and shut their traps.

Impressive!

I was the last to the party, having never been in the military myself, but I followed the lead of the others and brought myself into a full upright position.

Now all we need are some uniforms. Seriously, that would be wicked.

Charlie nodded to Daniel, his second in command, who was also our chief strategist. Daniel moved to the front and allowed his eyes to roam the room before speaking, ensuring he had our full regard. "As most of you know, Baylee and Matt excepted, we spent a good chunk of the afternoon discussing these very questions, and we think we have answers and a plan of attack.

"From flashes of memory seen in Krupert's head, we believe this key is black, and was created from a unique stone found on Perrin that is similar to your black diamond here on Earth. The missing four keys are most-likely precious

Perrinite stones in unique colors to differentiate from the others, but they will be similar in shape or design. For today our focus remains on finding this first key. Be advised, it may not look like a standard key; it could be any number of shapes, but if Krupert's memory serves, it will be under six inches in length.

"The consensus is that the key is buried somewhere in the tunnel under the house that Wrath was guarding. Between the destruction of the King's tether and our rescue of Merle and Krupert—triggering an alarm, if you remember—odds are good that the house will be crawling with black ninja types by now. In fact, we must assume they are lying in wait for us at this very moment.

"The only thing playing in our favor is that they believe—after 18 years of tortured test subjects—that their mindblock is foolproof. If they have no idea that we know anything about a key, there's a good chance their arrogance will lead them to leave it in place while they wait for our next move."

"So, we go in tomorrow during daylight hours, then?" I questioned, dreading the answer I knew was coming.

"Unfortunately, no," Daniel replied. "We've still got about an hour of light left today; we need to get in there now while odds are good the key remains. We've gathered supplies, and will have half the team slip in first in animal form. The other half will stay in human form and fight with Baylee, Charlie, and Randulf.

"Do I have two volunteers to stay behind with Candice and the animals?"

Bradley and Tara stepped forward. Tara was valuable as a medic, so she usually stayed behind in dangerous situations to care for any wounded, and Bradley was an excellent all-around defender and problem solver. His skills would be crucial if the house came under attack from Phoebus' men, and we could rule nothing out at this juncture.

Daniel took the two aside for a brief pow-wow, while those of us staying in human form flashed upstairs to don our own ninja attire. I pulled on the same black pants and shirt I'd worn the last time, decidedly lacking in ninja wear.

If we live through tonight, I am SO shopping at Ninjas-R-Us for better apparel. I wanta look badass like those evil ninjas. And then I could just tack on a ferocious dog and cat pin to differentiate me from the bad guys...ha!

Smith, Matt, Daniel, Charlie, Randulf and I remained as humans, while Krupert, Merle, Curtis, Rebecca, Ruth, and Jake quickly changed into their animal counterparts. It was kinda awesome seeing a rat, a bunny, and four cats sitting patiently side by side, and it gave me a weird sense of hope that if we could get through this, maybe everyone could learn to live together more harmoniously.

Smith flashed the whole group to the alleyway, where we peeked around the corner to examine the house. The sun was just starting to go down, so visibility was still within reasonable parameters, yet would quickly nosedive. We had to hurry.

The King and Charlie took on setting up a perimeter mindchime (sound buffer) and a mindunwind (attention-shifting buffer) so the neighborhood would remain unaware of what could soon be a large amount of activity here.

Seeing nothing untoward, Daniel gave the go-ahead to proceed with the plan. Smith whipped out his tools, and he and the animals flashed to the furthest basement window, where he quietly sliced a circle in the glass and the critters slipped through one by one and back into the dungeon.

I felt bad for Krupert and Merle, given that they'd spent the last six months trapped in a very special hell in that basement. I'm sure it was the last place they wanted to revisit, and I was worried they'd slip into a meltdown just by seeing it. But we needed their stealth and small size to scout for us; plus, they knew what they were getting themselves into, they were grown-butt men, so I pushed my concerns aside.

Every member of the team was tethered to Charlie's group mindlink, even the King and I, for ease of communication. We would all immediately know if anyone was in danger and could flash to him or her quickly.

Randulf, Charlie, Daniel, Matt, and I spent an anxious 60 seconds waiting for news from the first team. Smith flashed back to our side, reporting that he hadn't noted any movement from inside.

Suddenly Merle's voice came through the link "Oh, my God, NO!" his scream was shrill and terrifying, and I panicked, immediately flashing myself to the basement, although it was not in the plan and I knew I'd get chewed out later. *If I survive.*

My eyes took a second to adjust, but as they did I saw Merle locked in the constrictors of a massive python, a Perrin operative in snake form sent to take out our advance team. Krupert was climbing the snake's back and gnashing at him in an effort to save the rabbit, while the four cats tag-teamed him, slashing and biting at the snake from every angle.

They didn't seem to be making much progress, though, against such a formidable foe.

Well-played, Phoebus.

The rest of the team had flashed in behind me, and Smith's

keen eye promptly assessed the situation. He whipped out a small drill from his handyman backpack, jumping on the back of the snake and wasting no time in taking down the operative with a nasty but well-placed bit of machinery work. *Damn, he's righteous.*

As the snake collapsed to the ground, Merle fell with him and lay limp, no longer breathing.

No, no! I fell to the earthen floor alongside him and performed six sets of CPR, then flashed him back to Tara where I again repeated the life-saving technique, hoping if we could just keep his lungs and heart moving long enough for his body to start to heal he'd be ok. I laid him in Tara's arms and rushed back to the battle scene.

By the time I arrived, mayhem ruled.

I counted five ninjas and three more pythons, all in varying stages of deadly interactions with my friends, my family. I was again frozen with fear, not knowing where to go or who to help, and woefully ill-prepared for the mental anguish of war.

I knew we couldn't allow any more of our guys to get squeezed by the deadly snakes, but Smith and Matt were handling the first python, Matt acting as bait while Smith climbed its back with his trusty drill bit. The four cats and the rat terrorized and taunted the other two snakes, keeping them busy and away from the rest of us until Smith and Matt could work their magic.

I pulled my attention from them just as Charlie plunged into my head, "Behind you, Baylee!"

I turned in time to witness a ninja leaping for my back, a tether similar to Wrath's at the ready to slip over my neck. *WTF!* "Oh, Hells to the No," I screamed. *I'm not goin' feral again!* The red-hot power immediately zipped from my toes to my pelvis, igniting the kundalini energy coiled and ready to jump into action at the base of my spine. The bright yellow light burst forth from my solar plexus, slashing from me to the ninja and slamming him backward into the wall. The tether he'd managed to place halfway over my head became a lightning rod, jolting the yellow force from me back to him and frying him on the spot. He slumped to the ground.

I yanked the chain from my neck and swung it clumsily at the next ninja running toward me, desperation to keep her from killing or kidnapping me a potent ally. It arced gracelessly, flopping from my arm and randomly twisting through the air, by sheer coincidence connecting with her chest and zapping her with my sunbeam too. Her body flew up in the air and landed in a heap near the first guy.

Holy crap! An electric whip!

I didn't know if these guys were dead or just deep-fried unconscious, but I'd have to deal with that part later. I told myself I couldn't naively believe there would be no death when we were fighting such unsavory creatures; I had to put my team and myself first if we had any chance of saving both dimensions.

I flashed to Charlie's side where he was finishing off the last of the ninjas, fashioning makeshift handcuffs out of the guy's tether and trussing him up by both the arms and legs. That guy wasn't going anywhere without assistance anytime soon.

Randulf had turned into Wrath sometime during the attack, and stood over the mangled body of one of the ninjas as his German shepherd counterpart. He growled low in his throat as if claiming his kill, and I made a mental note to sign him up for a teensy bit of PTSD counseling at my earliest convenience.

His appointment could be right before mine. *Back away... back very far away from the crazy shepherd now, Bay.*

The final ninja lay unmoving near Daniel, and Matt and Smith had just made short work of the last snake.

We stood and circled as a group, backs to the center, watching closely for any new or emerging visible threats. Seeing none, Smith and Matt agreed to see to the bodies, disposing of the dead and confining those still alive for questioning.

The rest of us searched the basement for the key, our cat and rat teammates remaining in animal form to explore every inch—high and low—of the area.

With the aid of Krupert's superior sniffer we finally found a latch that swung a wall open to the expected tunnel, but despite covering every square foot of it we had come up empty-handed.

We had no idea if or when Phoebus would be sending reinforcements, and we needed to find that key and get out of there. Quick. We were spending way too much time in that basement, and it made us all jittery.

Wrath, Charlie and I moved to investigate the backyard for clues. If Wrath was outside and the key was inside—or under the house in a tunnel—it would be a little tough for him to actually guard it. So, what if the key was somewhere in his area instead, and the house and tunnel were just a decoy and a dumping ground for unwanted items like Merle and Krupert?

Upon entering the space which had imprisoned him for so many years, Wrath stumbled and fell, hit with another surge of PTSD.

His subdued voice explained to Charlie and I through the link that when he'd faced off with the ninja tonight, his dog counterpart remembered the man's scent. He was overcome with flashbacks of a dark-haired man taunting him, taking his food away, dumping his water. Leaving him starving and thirsty for weeks on end, laughing at him as he suffered and languished at the end of his chain.

When the memory surfaced the resulting trauma had forced his switch from immortal to shepherd form, and the thirst for revenge consumed him. He'd relentlessly attacked the man way past the point of death, ripping his throat out and feeling not a moment of remorse about it.

Sharing his unspeakable treatment at the hands of this man with us sent him into another fit of rage, and he ripped the doghouse to shreds, yanking the anchor stake from the ground in his frenzy.

As the post was wrenched from the soil, a hinge creaked, announcing the presence of a rusty doorway which sprung open to reveal a set of rickety steps leading to an underground chamber. *This is it, I can feel it!*

Wrath stopped dead in his tracks and the three of us looked at each other, stupefied. We dashed to the stairs, all thoughts on my part of containing Wrath's beast forgotten. Truth was, without his bout of destructive fury we'd have never found this place.

The room was large for a hideaway, measuring a good 12' x 12', and even featured a smelly port-a-john in the corner… obviously someone had spent considerable time down here. The walls were sloppily cemented overtop of the packed soil, and the spare furnishings consisted of a power supply, a laptop, a desk, and three cots, lined up side by side to save space. Beside the desk there was a small cabinet that held a mini fridge, a water cooler, and a microwave.

We called for Curtis through the comm link, and he flashed to us, excited to get his hands wet breaking through the laptop security while we continued to search for the key. Charlie fetched him and Randulf a set of clothes while they transformed back, and then we sectioned the room off into search quadrants.

As luck would have it, I drew the not-so-lucky latrine straw, and the gang about busted a gut laughing at me crawling around the reeking toilet looking for that ever-elusive black diamond key.

If they think I'm sticking my hand in that john hole and feelin' around, they definitely have another think comin'.

Ten minutes and no fortune cookie later, we stood in frustration, pondering where we went from here. We were considering admitting defeat and flashing home when Curtis yelled "I'm in!" and the laptop whirred to life, simultaneously lighting up and rolling back a panel along the wall to reveal a built-in cabinet and four monitors. *Whoa!*

Randulf lunged for the cabinet while the rest of us vied for space behind him. There was a tense moment while he searched and we waited for news, and then he whooped with delight and turned to us, clutching a clear glass case that held none other than a shiny black stone, cut into the shape of a chess king.

We did it. We found the first key!

No sooner had I exhaled a relieved sigh than the four monitors blipped on, each displaying ongoing live footage of emaciated dogs dragging heavy logging chains.

Randulf stopped mid-celebration and leaned heavily onto the only chair in the room.

His eyes roved from one monitor to the next, his hand covering his mouth as if to suppress the pain, hold it inside. Tears coursed down his cheeks as he visually devoured each dog.

He'd found his warriors.

One of the monitors panned close onto a massive Akita, his chocolate brown eyes gazing directly into the camera lens. I felt his stare as if he were reaching a tether directly into my soul.

Despite his skeletal state, he was the most magnificent creature I'd ever envisaged. I shivered, every hair on my body standing to attention, and one word reverberated throughout my mind.

"Mate."

My vision darkened and my world retracted; I would remember only a final grasp for connection as I lost consciousness, crumpling at Randulf's feet.

EPILOGUE

I awoke in my own bed, confused and shivering. There was not a sound in the house, and the pre-dawn glow of sunrise crept into my room through the open shutters.

But I was not alone. My father slept slouched in the chair beside me, his hand resting on my comforter as if to provide moral support. Despite my disorientation, a small smile lit my face at the sight of his rumpled clothing and bed head.

I knew my mother. Always before she had been by my side in times of trouble, but today she'd given Randulf the gift of parenthood.

And she'd given me the gift of knowing I had a father who would show up from this day forward.

Despite the challenges I faced in the upcoming months, I now had a foundation of parental love to build on, something far too few 18 year olds were blessed with. I knew I was lucky, and I hoped I would never forget, never take it for granted.

I tried to focus on my newly-whole family and not on the brown eyes of the Akita and the connection I'd felt so deeply it'd fried my circuitry.

Yet, my solar plexus had other ideas, pushing me in search of my soul-tether and sending my head spinning again as it sought out the bond.

I caught a break only in that I was already lying down.

I was suddenly held fast in the grip of a vision that was sharp, clear, and over in seconds.

I snapped out of it and sprang to a sitting position. I knew where we needed to go next.

And my family is not going to like it.

We hope you enjoyed Tamira Thayne's
The Wrath of Dog.

COULD YOU TAKE A MOMENT TO GIVE HER BOOK
A SHORT REVIEW ON AMAZON.COM? YOUR REVIEWS
MEAN THE WORLD TO OUR AUTHORS, AND HELP THEM
EXPAND THEIR AUDIENCE AND THEIR VOICE.
THANK YOU SO MUCH!

Find links to The Wrath of Dog and all our great books
on Amazon or at www.whochainsyou.com.

ACKNOWLEDGMENTS

Thank you to my beta readers, Laura, Liz, and Cayr, for the insightful feedback and ideas on *Wrath of Dog* in addition to the outstanding grammar help. Any remaining errors are solely on me.

I also wish to express my gratitude to the other authors at Who Chains You Books for your camaraderie and belief in our joint publishing efforts. Working with you all warms my heart and makes getting out of bed in the morning worthwhile.

I wouldn't be the person I am today without the chained dogs and the many friends I've made who still work the front lines for the voiceless. I know these poor dogs deserve better, and I can only pray someday all humans get the memo. It is a "No-Brainer" after all.

Special thanks to Melody Whitworth, founder of Unchained Melodies Dog Rescue (unchainedmelodies.org), and Deb Carr, former treasurer of Dogs Deserve Better. I couldn't have any more respect for you ladies than I do: my heart sisters.

All my love to my hubby Joe for supporting me and standing by my side through some very interesting adventures, and my kids, Rayne and Bryn, who always hold half my heart.

Last but never least, special love to my real-life current animal family: Khronos, Una, Tootie, Vivian, BooBoo, Tika, and all the outside critters I admire and care for.

Tamira Thayne pioneered the anti-tethering movement in America, forming and leading the nonprofit Dogs Deserve Better for 13 years.

During her time on the front lines of animal activism and rescue she took on plenty of bad guys (often failing miserably); her swan song culminated in the purchase and transformation of Michael Vick's dogfighting compound to a chained-dog rescue and rehabilitation center. She's spent 878 hours chained to a doghouse on behalf of the voiceless in front of state capitol buildings nationwide, and worked with her daughter to take on a school system's cat dissection program, garnering over 100,000 signatures against the practice.

She's the author of the Chained Gods series, the Animal Protectors Series, *Foster Doggie Insanity* and *Capitol in Chains*. She's the editor of *More Rescue Smiles*, and the co-editor of *Unchain My Heart* and *Rescue Smiles*.

In 2016 she founded Who Chains You, publishing books by and for animal activists and rescuers.

Also from Tamira Thayne

THE CURSE OF CUR: THE CHAINED GODS SERIES BOOK 2

An animal activist teenager continues her quest to save two dimensions in this sequel to *The Wrath of Dog...*

Baylee couldn't afford to be sidetracked from her vision— the vision that told her they needed to get to New York City, and fast.

Because she knew where the Akita they'd seen on screen yesterday, her father's second in command, was chained...

Now it was time for Baylee, her father, and Perrin's remaining top generals to buck up. It was her mission, their collective mission, to find the chained warriors, unearth the remaining four keys, and rescue both Perrin and Earth from the grip of Phoebus, The Scion, and their legion of minions.

Easy peasy.

Baylee leaned heavily against the bathroom wall, toothbrush hanging from her mouth. Oh, who was she kidding.

The future looked daunting, indeed....*Read more and order from whochainsyou.com, Amazon, and other outlets.*

Also from Tamira Thayne

THE KING'S TETHER:
A CHAINED GODS SERIES PREQUEL STORY

In a rare moment of inactivity, the dog rested his head on his front paws. The thick logging chain weighed heavily across his body as he pulled his back legs from beneath the oppressive steel. His eyelids drooped, and even though his feral mind urged him to remain vigilant, told him he was in constant danger, sleep had its way with him anyway.

With sleep came relief.

In the waking state his mind knew only bloodlust and revenge, his body hunger and thirst, and his heart pain and sorrow. In slumber his consciousness freed itself from its bonds, and he revisited an immortal life once known—only to lose the beloved memories upon reawakening.

The ultimate cruelty.

A kick to the ribs lurched him from the dream, and his past slipped away from him, again...*Read more and order from whochainsyou.com, Amazon, and other outlets.*

Also from Tamira Thayne

THE KNIGHTS CHAIN:
A CHAINED GODS SERIES STORY

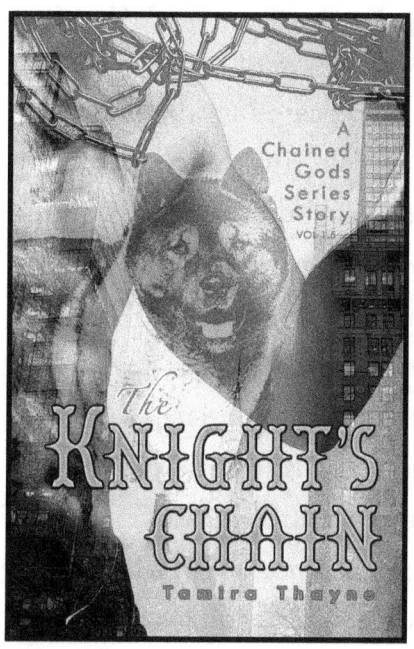

The Akita was massive, a fine example of the breed—with the single exception of his current physical state: skeletal, matted, and attached to a cement post by a thick logging chain. He refused to let those things bother him, however; they were mere nuisances, after all.

What mattered most to him was that any of his captors—the men in black—who crossed his path would die.

Simple as that.

He was done with the torture, had enough of the domination. His mind may have been jumbled, with memories of the past escaping him—but he knew one thing for sure: he was more than this beast on a chain. For now, he would wait...

The Knight's Chain, a short story, precedes *The Curse of Cur*, and can be read before Book 2 of The Chained Gods Series or after to flesh out the character of the Knight.....*Read more and order from whochainsyou.com, Amazon, and other outlets.*

Also from Tamira Thayne

FOSTER DOGGIE INSANITY: TIPS AND TALES TO KEEP YOUR KOOL AS A DOGGIE FOSTER PARENT

Have you ever fostered a dog—happy to make a difference—but wondered why you felt frustrated and alone in your experience? Do you want to foster a dog, but don't know where to start, how to prepare, and what to expect? Have you experienced burnout or compassion fatigue in your rescue experience? If so, this is the book for you. Described as "an embrace from a friend who understands what we all go through; it is a beacon of hope to let other rescuers know they are not alone—a must-read for anyone involved in rescue."

This is not a book about dog training, but a book about people training while working with dogs...*Read more and order from whochainsyou.com, Amazon, and other outlets.*

About Who Chains You Books

WELCOME TO WHO CHAINS YOU: PUBLISHING AND SPIRITUAL MENTORING FOR ANIMAL ACTIVISTS AND ANIMAL RESCUERS.

Who Chains You Publishing brings the work of animal activists and rescuers to your doorstep through books highlighting successes, missteps, and the brightest imaginative endeavors of those who love animals and fight on their behalf.

Animal activists and rescuers find ourselves at the forefront of THE social issue of modern times. The last hundred years have seen major leaps for women's rights, racial equality, and—most recently—gay rights. Even the animals have gained some ground. But, unfortunately, we have a LONG way to go for true freedom for those who remain voiceless in our society.

We hope you'll visit our website and join us on this adventure we call animal advocacy publishing. We welcome you.

Read more about us at whochainsyou.com.

www.ingramcontent.com/pod-product-compliance
Lightning Source LLC
Chambersburg PA
CBHW072233170626
46813CB00003B/1207